Gorgeous George
And The Giant Geriatric Generator

Stuart Reid

Illustrations & Cover by Calvin Innes

Copyright © My Little Big Town Ltd 2011

Hessle . East Yorkshire . HU13 9DG

First Print 2011

ISBN: 1907746021
ISBN-13: 978-1-907746-02-4

www.mylittlebigtown.com/gorgeousgeorge

DEDICATION

For my girls. Audrey for encouraging the madness, Jess for living it and Charley for adding the magic.

CONTENTS

ACKNOWLEDGMENTS

From the imagination of
Stuart Reid

Artwork, doodles and characters by
Calvin Innes

Chopped and changed by
Linda Innes

I. THE SHADOWS

George was wide awake.

There was a thick fog outside which seemed to glimmer orange in the street-lights. A glow was twinkling through the frost that was forming on the outside of the window and George lay in his bed, mesmerized by the sparkles through a gap in the curtains.

Almost hypnotised, George slipped out of bed, crept toward the window and parted the curtains ever so slightly.

The street outside was wrapped in a cold blanket of mist and only the street-lights could be seen, like large balls of flickering amber. The rest of the street was either painted with a light orange glow, or hidden in pitch black shadow.

George sat for a long time and watched the icicle shapes grow on his window. Crystal fingers stretched inwards from the edges of the glass; crisp and sharp, forming intricate designs as tiny droplets of water began to freeze and expand with the rapidly dropping night-time temperatures.

There was no noise in the street; it was completely silent as if the fog had smothered any sound that dared to creep out from the darkness.

But if George strained his ears hard enough and closed his eyes tightly, there, right on the corner of his imagination he was certain he could hear a low humming noise. Not quite a groaning or a growling but a soft humming whirl coming from outside.

His house was silent. Everyone would be sleeping soundly, the heating had switched itself off hours ago and all the plugs were pulled out of their sockets. Apart from George, nothing moved inside his house. The noise had to be coming from outside.

The humming sound was darting along the edges of his imagination now. Curiosity and intrigue dared George to open the window, just a tiny bit, to hear the sound a little clearer.

As soon as George turned the handle and pushed quietly an icy blast of cold air rushed into his bedroom and he shivered inside his pyjamas. George's breath blew puffy clouds out towards the small gap in the window frame and he pulled his arms tightly around his body. Settling down on his knees he closed his eyes again and concentrated on the humming sound.

The noise was definitely not in his imagination now; it was outside, down the bottom of the street and coming closer. George opened his eyes and strained to see through the amber mist into the darkness beyond. The humming was always there.

At the very bottom of the street, where the houses meet the park and the large trees and hedges absorb all the street-lights, George saw two eyes approaching through the darkness. These eyes burned softly with a bluish white radiance that split through the orange fog.

As these two eyes slid closer up the street, George saw that they were the headlights of a small truck; an almost silent little box on four wheels, painted a dull black colour which absorbed all the light around it. And as the little black truck coasted up the middle of the road, George realised that this was where the humming noise was coming from.

It wasn't a noisy petrol motor like a car or a coughing spluttering diesel engine that was powering the black truck; it seemed to George that a noiseless, unseen hand was pushing the strange vehicle along.

George had heard his Grandpa Jock talk about the old days, when people had their milk delivered directly onto their doorstep, straight from the dairy, without even sniffing a supermarket. Milk was delivered in little trucks called milk-floats. Grandpa Jock said these milk-floats had electric motors and the reason they were called milk-floats was because these little trucks were so quiet that they seemed to float along the road, without a sound.

But nobody in Little Pumpington gets milk delivered to their doorstep now, not unless it's been ordered online and usually comes along with lots of other groceries from the big supermarket inside your computer. And nobody has their shopping delivered at one o'clock in the morning.

So George was pondering the mystery of a midnight milk merchant when the truck bumped up onto the pavement and stopped outside old Mr Swan's house.

Mr Swan was a grouchy old man who smelled a little bit like wee and a lot like stale beer. George's dad said that when Mr Swan dies, they'd better not cremate him or he'll go up like Guy Fawkes although George wasn't quite sure what he'd meant.

Mr Swan always wore three jerseys and a cardigan, even in the summer, and in the winter he'd wear special gloves with the fingertips cut off them. George thought that this was so Mr Swan could keep his hands warm and still pick his nose, which was quite a good idea because when George wore gloves and picked his nose, the fluffy fingertips were always getting gummed up with bogies, the wool made his nose tickle and his mum usually went mad, shouting 'I hope this snot comes off in the wash!'.

George always sniggered when he thought about his bogies swimming around in the same washing machine as his dad's favourite golf sweater.

But George wasn't sniggering now. George was shivering and not with the cold. He had seen two enormous shadows step out of the black truck and go in through the front door of Mr Swan's house. These shadows lurched, rather than walked and had a sinister sense of purpose. Two minutes later the shadows returned, this time staggering more than swaggering as they carried a large, black sack. They disappeared behind the truck and George saw one of the vehicle's back doors open, then softly close again without a sound. One of the dark shadows appeared around this side of the truck, opened the driver's door and was about to step in, then paused. The shadow looked up at George's window and their eyes met. At least George's eyes met with an evil glint from inside a black hood and George seemed too paralysed to move, his body was tingling all over and he held his breath.

Holding his breath seemed a good idea because George thought that maybe the shadow had seen the warm, cloudy air billowing out from his mouth and escaping through the gap in the window that was still open a few inches. Gulp!

The shadow lifted its large club of a clenched fist and with a stiff, dagger-like thumb drew its hand across its neck. George didn't hear if this was accompanied with a creaking, tearing sound from the back of the shadow's throat but it should have been and probably was; only the fog had stifled it.

'GEORGE!'

George leapt into the air, his heart missing a beat at the shout and he turned toward his bedroom door.

George's mum flew into the room in a flurry, with the frustrated annoyance of a parent who didn't want to get up out of their nice, warm bed but knew that they had to.

'What are you doing out of bed at this time? Why is your window open?' she asked, 'have you been sleep walking again?'

'No, mum, it's the shadows,' George replied sleepily and he turned to the window to see the street, empty, orange and completely quiet again.

'Shadows? Really George!' George's mum muttered as she stepped over and pulled the window tight shut. 'Get back into bed and no more silly dreaming. You and your imagination boy.' And she bundled George into his bed, pulled the quilt around him and tucked it under his legs.

'Now go to sleep.' And she scurried off to her bedroom again, hoping that the duvet was as warm and snuggly as it had been when she'd left it two minutes earlier but knowing that it never was. George closed his eyes and wondered if he really had been dreaming as the swaggering, staggering shadows lumbered around the edges of his mind and he slowly drifted off to sleep.

II. THE HISTORY OF THE POWER PLANT

Nearly one hundred years ago, in Little Pumpington, a power plant was founded by three men called Mr. Peabody, Mr. Percival and Mr. Prickly. These founding members decided to name their power plant after themselves, as many rich and pompous men do, and called their company 3P's Power.

The three Mister P's were mean, malicious men and wanted to do everything possible to make as much money as they could, as quickly as they were able. They employed children and paid them 2p a week and when child labour was banned by the government, they employed the poorest people in the town and continually threatened to fire them if they didn't work hard enough.

Now, even though the factory was a power plant, burning lots of coal and turning it into electricity, there were parts of the factory that could get quite cold in the winter. When some of the workers complained that they couldn't feel their fingers, Mr Peabody, Mr Percival and Mr Prickly agreed to turn the heating on in those parts of the plant. Then they docked everybody's wages to pay for the heat!

And it was a dirty job too. There was soot, smoke and
steam everywhere, especially at the bottom of the three
enormous chimney stacks. If you didn't work in the
freezing cold part of the factory, then you worked in the
boiler room, a swelteringly hot pit of fire and burning

coals, where the men fried eggs on their shovels for their lunch and when they walked around the corridors next to the gigantic coal-burning furnace, they splashed through deep puddles of their own sweat.

Thirty years after the power plant opened, Mr. Prickly suggested to Mr Peabody that his son Peter should marry Mr. Peabody's daughter Patricia. That way all the money that they made stayed in their family and they didn't have to share it with anyone. (Mr Percival had long since met an accident in the furnace of the factory, when he 'accidentally' tripped and fell into the giant oven, when inspecting the boiler room with Mr Peabody and Mr Prickly. There were no other witnesses.)

So Peter Prickly married Patricia Peabody and ten years later, they had a daughter whom they called Petunia, who became the sole heir to 3P's Power.

Now when Petunia was a young girl she used to visit her father, Mr. Prickly Junior at the power plant almost every day. She loved looking down from the big director's office and over-seeing the whole factory. To Petunia, it seemed like the most marvellous position of power, she loved the feeling of control it seemed to give her over the 'little' workers running about down below on the factory floor. She would tour the factory with her father, who would shout at his struggling labourers to work harder or to stop slacking. He showed Petunia how power plants burned fossil fuels like coal and oil, boiling water like a giant kettle and turning it into steam, which then fuelled a generator which stored the power until it was needed; usually when the people of Little Pumpington turned on their TV's and lights at home, especially in the evening.

There was one part of the tour that Petunia hated and this was when they walked through the basement where the engines churned and generators rumbled loudly and the valves hissed and spat steam everywhere and cranking of the pipes was so loud she could hardly hear herself speak. Petunia hated the noise.

Over the years, Petunia visited the factory less and less as her school-work and studies took over. She left school and went to college to become a teacher, imagining the power and control she could wield over whole classrooms full of little people.

One summer's day during the school holidays, Petunia returned to the factory to visit her father once more.

'Aren't you inspecting the factory today, father?' she asked, wondering if she should take the tour again with her father for old times sake, but secretly thinking that she didn't really want to see the dirty old furnaces one more time.

'No, my dear,' wheezed Mr Prickly Jr. pompously 'I've found a marvellous young foreman to do all that work. I never need to set foot out of this office.' And Mr Prickly Jr. coughed, wretched and cleared his throat in one hacking breath. 'His name is young Mr Watt and I think you'll rather like him'

Mr Prickly Jr. pointed out of his office window to a smart young man, quite tall, with broad shoulders in a brown suit, marching through the factory floor with a clipboard. By the time Petunia had left her father's office and stepped down the long flight of stairs to the factory floor, she saw Mr Watt pointing his finger in a poor worker's chest and shouting at him.

'You're fired!' he bellowed and Petunia fell in love with him immediately. His forceful, bullying manner was just like her father's and she knew she wanted to spend the rest of her life with this young man, whether he wanted to spend it with her or not.

What Petunia did not know about Mr Watt was that he had a dream too. He longed to own his own power plant. He loved the factory and its marvellous ability to turn coal into energy; how this had transformed the lives of everyone in Little Pumpington and most importantly, Mr Watt loved the feeling of control this gave him over everyone's lives. He wanted to control everything too, a bit like Petunia.

When he was a small boy, Mr Watt had enjoyed frying the wings off insects with his magnifying glass or putting fireworks up cats' bottoms. Not only was this very cruel but people kept finding crispy bits of cats' fur fluttering around the streets for days after fireworks night. And of course, the cats weren't too happy about the idea either.

As he grew older, Mr Watt's sense of manipulation and domination grew with him until he found it was not enough that he succeeded, everyone else must also fail. As soon as he left school, he enrolled in Power Plant Academy to learn all about power, energy and electricity and his control freakery started to take over his studies.

In order to guarantee he scored the highest marks in the end of term exams, Mr Watt studied longer and harder than any other student in the final few days leading up to the exams, sometimes working well into the night. After dark, Mr Watt's light could always be seen burning in his dormitory and occasionally he was forced to take a moonlight stroll to clear his head before falling asleep.

Mr Watt refused to drink water before the exams, insisting that he'd been studying so long and so hard that all he needed to drink was cola and caffeine energy drinks, straight out of a can just to stay awake.

And this was indeed a massive stroke of good fortune for Mr Watt because, and no one ever found out exactly how this happened but the mains water supply that flowed into Power Plant Academy and dormitory had become polluted with a tasteless, yet powerful laxative and all the students sitting the energy exams were struck down with the most violent bouts of diarrhoea.

People were forced to rush out of the examination hall to the toilet every ten minutes and at times there was a bit of a log jam in the bathrooms. There would be queues of students, crossing their legs and clenching their bottom cheeks, waiting for the next cubicle to become free. The drains became clogged up and one or two didn't quite make it to the toilet in time.

By the end of the exam, the hall had become a very smelly place but fortunately for Mr Watt, who'd kept drinking his energy drink and hadn't touched the water, he remained sitting at his desk throughout the examination and successfully completed all the questions within the time limit.

Mr Watt graduated top of his class quite easily, since most of the other students didn't even finish their papers, and the next stage of his plan to become the best power plant manager ever was put into place. He then applied directly to 3P's Power for a job, enclosing with his letter, not only his exam results but a league table of all the students' marks.

Mr. Prickly Jr. had noted Mr Watt's excellent results, especially compared to his other classmates, and when he interviewed Mr Watt, Mr Prickly Jr. was also very impressed with Mr. Watt's air of authority and natural command, so before he'd even arrived at the factory to start his new job Mr. Watt had been promoted to foreman.

After that, Petunia, who, as a spoilt little rich girl had her father twisted around her finger, convinced him of Mr Watt's talent, abilities and desires. Whilst he was courting young Petunia Prickly, Mr Watt, always with an eye for opportunity, was promoted by Mr Prickly Jr. to the role of director.

The following year, after Mr. Watt married Miss Petunia, her father promoted Mr Watt to the lofty position of Managing Director. Old Mr. Prickly Jr. promptly retired, then died. In the space of two short years Mr Watt had gained total control of the 3P's Power where he remained as Managing Dictator, I mean Director, ruthlessly ruling over the power plant.

III. SCHOOL ON MONDAY MORNING

Today, George Hansen lived in the town of Little Pumpington, on the north east coast of England. George was ten years old and it always seemed rather odd to him that, although there was a small town called Little Pumpington, there wasn't a larger town called Big Pumpington or even a city called Great Big Pumpington. George always thought there should be.

George's Grandpa Jock had once told him that the reason why Little Pumpington was called Little Pumpington was because high on the hill overlooking the town was the power plant and every since the plant had been built, on the hour, every hour, one of the three chimneys at the plant would let out a gaseous 'parp' of foul smelling steam, which stunk like old cabbages. The factory didn't make that noise any more so George wasn't sure whether to believe his Grandpa Jock or not.

George lived in a small house with his mum and dad but not his big sister, Henrietta who was much older than George and had now gone off to college to study social sciences or something like that. 'University of Stating the Blooming Obvious!' Dad called it, muttering under his breath every time Henrietta phoned home to ask for more money.

'You should be glad she got into university,' Mum would scold him.

'She's lucky she didn't get into Skidmore College, her marks were so bad.' Dad would always chuckle after saying something like that, proud that he could amuse himself quietly.

That's probably where George got his sense of humour from. George was usually a quiet boy because he discovered that everybody else had their own opinion on things but most of the time they were wrong. George decided that he didn't want to talk with people who didn't share his correct opinion. Arguing always seemed like such a big waste of time too, especially when most people were usually wrong but were always too stupid to realise it. To George, it just felt like an enormous waste of energy to try to change the other person's minds.

So he didn't. He usually found it easier to keep quiet and simply ignore other people's opinions.

That morning, George had slept in for school. This was probably due to his late night window watching or sleep walking or whatever he had been up to. Had he been dreaming? Now George wasn't so sure and his memory was as foggy as the street had been last night so maybe his mum was right.

George was now wolfing down his last piece of toast and trying to drink his milk. His mum was thrusting one of his arms into the sleeve of his jacket.

'Come on, lad. Hurry up.' said his mum slipping his arm into the second sleeve and hooking the strap from his school bag across his wrist in one swift motion. George's toast became lost somewhere in the whole whirlwind.

Just then, George's dad stepped through the back door. 'Morning all.' he said cheerily, waving the newspaper at George and his mum. George's dad always woke up early and went out for a long walk first thing in the morning, before stopping off at the newsagents on the way home.

'I hear Mr Swan's off to Florida, dear.' Mr Hansen said.

'That'll be nice for him,' replied George's mum, 'nice bit of sunshine at this time of year. How did you hear about that then?'

Mr Hansen scratched his head, 'That's the funny thing,' he said, 'Mr Russell at the paper shop said that one of his paper boys found a note on his doorstep this morning, saying he was off to Florida and to cancel his papers.'

'That was sudden,' replied Mrs Hansen, 'but you never can tell with old people these days. It seems as fast as an idea comes into their heads, they're off. Take Mr Higginbottom, who shot off on a worldwide cruise last year, suddenly decided it was his life long ambition. And look at old Mrs Davies a few years back. Off to visit her friend in Badger's Creek. Without even telling anyone! I mean, who would guess that that mean old bat had any friends?'

'Maybe Grandpa Jock might want to rush off back to Scotland next.' George's mum laughed and George thought that she looked a little bit too happy at the prospect.

'And then there was that coach load of pensioners who wanted to be missionaries in Africa. Remember that, about four or five years ago?' added George's dad. 'They never came back again, did they?'

Then it dawned on George. He stopped in his tracks. 'Mr Swan's gone?' he asked, starting to feel a shiver of concern, ever so slightly, and raising one eyebrow.

'Yes, apparently,' said Dad. 'left yesterday, according to his note.'

'But what about the shadows I saw going into his house last night?' squealed George.

'Oh, you and your shadows!' groaned his mother. 'That imagination will get you in trouble one day, boy.' And with that she forced him out of the house and pushed him off in the direction of the school, whilst pulling out a half-eaten, slightly soggy piece of toast from the hood of George's jacket.

So George was running late for school that morning, slightly hungry due to his lack of toast, slightly sleepy due to his late night vigil and slightly grouchy for being rushed out of his house. George was also concerned about Mr Swan.

He didn't like Mr Swan much, and might even be a bit scared of him, (though George would never admit to that) but he didn't like the thought of someone being dragged out of the house in the middle of the night, in an old sack by two shadowy thugs. Even though he was late, George meandered slowly to school, thinking over last night's events and what his dad had told him this morning.

It didn't seem likely. It didn't seem possible. But it seemed less likely and more impossible that Mr Swan had been kidnapped from his own bed by two masked hoods driving the stealth bomber equivalent of a milk-float; these things just don't happen in towns like Little Pumpington, or anywhere else for that matter.

'Good afternoon, George,' Mrs Watt spat out sarcastically. 'Sit down immediately and try to arrive here on time tomorrow.' George was last into the class room but the bell had only rung 30 seconds ago so he felt that Mrs Watt was being a little unfair.

Mrs Watt was George's teacher. Mrs Petunia Watt, formerly Miss Prickly. Old Mrs Watt, as she was sometimes known. Evil old bag-face Watt, less so. Mrs

Moaning-Faced-Sucking-on-a-Lemon-would-be-an-improvement-and-probably-too-good-for-her-Watt, as only George liked to call her.

Mrs Petunia Watt wasn't actually that old, she just seemed to have been around forever and had done her very best, throughout her career as a teacher, to suck all the fun and enjoyment out of every subject and student that came within a 10 metre radius of her classroom, leaving nothing but a shrivelled, dry husk of educated matter. Mrs Watt's idea of good schooling was to educate a child to within an inch of their life, whether they wanted to be taught or not. George had even overheard Mrs Watt telling one of the student teachers that 'Doing away with the cane was the worst education decision ever. The cane only forces the knowledge deeper.' she announced with some passion.

Now again, Grandpa Jock's knowledge of all things ancient helped George out with this one. George had never heard of the cane before. Apparently the cane was a piece of bamboo about one metre long and it made a vicious 'whippy' sound when you swished it around. The cane, or in Scotland where Grandpa Jock went to school, a leather belt, was used to beat small children who talked in class or didn't understand the question or spelt a word wrong on their homework. Bad teachers used the cane all the time to prove how much discipline and education they were instilling in their pupils. Grandpa Jock said good teachers didn't really use the cane much but some of them liked to keep it on display, as a constant threat.

George sat down in his regular seat at the back of the classroom. He sat on his own at a double desk in the corner and George liked sitting at the back because if he stayed quiet and kept his head down, Mrs Watt would sometimes forget he was there and he could allow his thoughts to drift off to the bottom of the ocean or to outer space where he could conjure up new creatures, living in strange lands or anywhere George's imagination wanted to take him.

This morning however, Mrs Watt stood at the front of the class, tall and very slim, with her beady eyes peering out over the top of her half moon glasses, staring at George.

'Boys and girls,' she began, making the words sound like poop on her shoe, 'this is Allison, Allison Lansbury. Now Allison and her mother have just moved to Little Pumpington and she'll be joining this class. Make her feel welcome or else.'

Allison had short brown hair and big blue eyes. Her skin was slightly tanned and she held her head straight up looking at the back of the class and not wishing to make eye contact with anyone. She sighed with a bored expression on her face which changed immediately when Mrs Watt looked down at her. Suddenly Allison smiled sweetly and Mrs Watt's puzzled eyes couldn't be quite sure if she was being made a fool of.

'You can sit at the back, beside George. Off you go.' said Mrs Watt shoving Allison through the first row of desks. Allison breathed heavily again and sat down beside George.

'Hi.' she said quietly to George, as she sat down on the vacant chair.

'Hi you.' said George, not wishing to be rude but secretly annoyed that his empty, peaceful double desk was now shared with a girl.

'Is she always such a stuck-up dragon?' whispered Allison.

George sniggered loudly and Mrs Watt threw a marker pen at him, which bounced off his head and hit the window.

'Stop that nonsense, George,' yelled Mrs Watt, her face turning from its usual pale yellow colour to a more purple tinge, as the broken veins in her cheeks filled up with blood. 'You are to look after the new girl, not to show her how badly you can behave.'

Now George really was starting to lose his patience. Today was not turning out to be a good day since he got out of bed, on the right side but at the wrong time. He hadn't been able to finish his toast, his mum didn't believe him about Mr Swan's shadows, he'd lost his spacious double desk and now the lump on his head was starting to throb.

Things began to get worse when the first subject of the day was maths.

Mrs Watt drew a map on the board with four points laid out A, B, C and D in a semi circle, with her unique squiggly drawings of a bridge, a tree and something that looked like a car. The children giggled at her pictures and she gave them a dirty look over her shoulder.

Mrs Watt began to explain 'If a man leaves point A at 12pm and travels to point B at 30 miles an hour.......; George was soon beginning to switch off, he closed his eyes. Mrs Watt droned on and on and on.

'What is the quickest way from point A to point D?' asked Mrs Watt.

'Drive at the speed of light,' giggled Allison, nudging George.

'What was that?' shouted Mrs Watt and another marker pen flew across the classroom and caught a rather sleepy-eyed George on the tip of his ear. Years of practise at throwing chalk (a long time ago) and now marker pens at wayward children had ensured Mrs Watt had an aim as accurate as a darts player and she was deadly from 10 metres.

'George!' she shrieked, 'Were you sleeping in my class?'

'No, miss,' replied George, rubbing his eyes.

'Then what is the fastest route from point A to point D?'

Something stirred inside his head as he searched for the right answer. It seemed obvious, logical and somehow familiar. 'Drive at the speed of light, Miss?' George blurted out before his brain could engage second gear.

The class exploded into laughter and for the second time that morning, Mrs Watt's face began to take on a dangerous shade of plum. Then she relaxed, her shoulders settled and a malicious grin spread across her face.

That look was enough to quieten down any children who were still laughing at George's clumsy answer, as they all knew 'that look' was a forewarning of ridicule. Some teachers, especially the not very good ones and PE teachers, liked to use ridicule to stamp out any act of insubordination in their classrooms. George had seen this in other teachers, who he was sure, actually enjoyed making fools of unfortunate children, allowing the teacher to remain in control of the class and strike enough fear into the other pupils that they'd think twice about starting any mischief themselves. Mrs Watt wanted her classroom and the school to be a mischief-free zone.

No pupil ever wanted to be captured by 'that look'.

'So, George, you think you know what the speed of light is?' said Mrs Watt smugly, 'please inform the rest of the class.'

'Uuuuuuhm,' George stalled.

'Come now, young Mr Hansen,' declared Mrs Watt haughtily, 'please enlighten us with your infinite knowledge of the vastness of the Universe and its scientific principals.' Mrs Watt was in full humiliation mode, hoping to pull the rug out from under George's feet.

'Errrrrrrrm,' stalled George again.

'Or don't you know, Mr Hansen. Do you just blurt out the first thing that enters your empty, little head?' The class tittered.

But George wasn't stalling. He wasn't hesitating, pausing for thought or even wavering uncertainly around the periphery of his brain. George's head certainly wasn't empty; he knew the answer, or at least he thought he knew. Right at the back of George's mind was his bucket of knowledge that George filled with the stuff that interested him, only problem was that it took a few seconds to find the right information, after a bit of rooting around.

'One hundred and eighty-six thousand miles per second!' George shouted triumphantly, rather like a darts commentator on the telly.

For the second time that morning the classroom erupted into howls and shrieks of laughter at the preposterous way George announced his choice of answer to the class. Mrs Watt took this as her sign of victory and, even though she wasn't exactly sure of the correct answer herself, the mockery of the rest of George's classmates convinced her that he was wrong.

'One hundred and eighty-six thousand miles?' spluttered Mrs Watt, 'Per second!' and she slapped her hands against her legs and joined the rest of the class in uncontrolled laughter. Mrs Watt's laugh had a vicious, nasty edge to it.

'I think you mean 'per hour', boy!' sneered Mrs Watt.

Now George was well aware that it was wrong to argue with a teacher but he was absolutely convinced that the speed of light was one hundred and eighty six thousand miles per second, (which it is) and he wasn't going to allow his morning to get worse by admitting he was wrong.

Mrs Watt, on the other hand, couldn't believe it was 'per second' and tried to argue that it must be per hour simply because George thought the opposite. George was getting more and more agitated as he tried to tell Mrs Watt that he 'just knew', when she seriously started to belittle him.

'So George knows everything, doesn't know how or why. He just knows,' She scoffed, 'why are you so convinced that you just know?'

'Because, teachers don't always know everything!' George shouted and silence fell across the whole room.

Mrs Watt was shocked by this outburst and drew herself up to her full height, and turned to the rest of the children sitting in the classroom and announced,

'The trouble with George is that he always thinks he's right. If he was in the army and the other soldiers were marching 'left, right, left, right', George would be marching 'right, left, right, left' and still thinking he was correct.' She went on, 'George, you must accept that sometimes you are wrong. Detention!'

Again, George had learned a difficult lesson that it was better not argue his case than get into trouble for trying to prove his point. So again, George decided to stay silent.

George sat in class with his head held up on his hands, being careful not to close his eyes but allowing his mind to drift off to continue the argument with Mrs Watt. Obviously George would win this discussion almost immediately.

Without any heated exchange of words, as George's imagination carefully and quietly explained to the Mrs Watt exactly how he knew he was correct; that he'd read it in his Bumper Book of Science and his reasoning was beyond reproach. Imaginary Mrs Watt then gracefully conceded that her knowledge of science was not what it should be and bowed down to the superior power of the Bumper Book and George's flawless memory retention.

Then, moving quickly onto his next thought, again about Mrs Watt. 'Left, right, left, right, you think you are always right, George,'

George's mind was working overtime now. 'Well Mrs Watt, I believe I can be. If the soldiers you described were marching 'left, right, left, right' but their sergeant major was shouting 'right, left, right, left' then technically, I would be marching correctly and the rest of the squad would be in the wrong.'

Imaginary Mrs Watt once again conceded, 'I acknowledge your thoughtful strategy and superiority....'

George, closing his eyes lightly, gently nodded his head to accept his teacher's apology.

'Are you sleeping in my class again?' and George lifted his head quickly as another pen narrowly missed his cheek. 'What are you smiling about now, boy?' shouted Mrs Watt, unable to keep hold of her temper.

'Nothing, Mrs Watt.' George whispered.

'Well, you'd better not be or it will be double detention for you, Gorgeous George,' she spat. George felt his stomach cringe at his teacher's cruelty.

The problem was that George wasn't gorgeous. Even at best, George could only be described as almost averagely normal looking, in the right kind of light; if the right kind of light meant a little bit dull. His head was an ever-so-slightly-strange shape, it might be said, by someone who wanted to be nasty, that his face had been put together in the dark, by a one handed man who'd just been poked in the eye with a very sharp stick.

His nose was a little crooked, just a tiny bit. His mouth turned down ever so slightly at one side. One of his eyes was just a bit lower than the other and his ears stuck out, not much but enough for you to notice.

Individually all these things wouldn't have mattered too much but when they were all put together it gave George a slightly odd appearance. No-one could ever say exactly why they thought George looked like a badly put together Mr. Potato-Head, he just did.

So children being children, they teased and taunted him for being slightly different, never physically bullying him but reminding him in a cruel fashion that the only way he'd ever win 2nd prize in a beauty competition was if none of the other competitors turned up.

It was during an earlier real-life 'discussion' with an older girl over the price of a piece of cheese that she christened him 'Gorgeous George'. Everyone in the whole school laughed and the name had stuck ever since.

'Here comes Gorgeous George!' the girls would sing after that, and then the wolf-whistles would start, mocking George as he passed. Of course, what made it worse was that his surname was Hansen.

'Oooh, Gorgeous George Hansen.' one of the girls would squeal rudely.

'No, this is it. Gorgeous George Handsome.' the biggest girl would laugh and they would all start up a chorus of 'Gorgeous George Handsome, Handsome Gorgeous George!'

George always just kept his head held up and walked on, ignoring them and their nastiness.

Back in the classroom, Allison leaned over from her side of the double desk and whispered, 'Don't listen to that mean old witch. I think your face has got character.' and she squeezed George's arm under the desk.

George smiled to himself and felt his day get a whole lot better.

IV. MR WATT

George had lived in Little Pumpington all his life and those girls who laughed at him and the boys who called him names were not the only people who were horrid. It seemed that everybody in the town was always cruel or nasty to everyone else. No-one ever said 'please' or 'thank you'. People would barge past each other in the street and not even say sorry. Everyone was always in a rush. And everyone was permanently afraid of losing their job or worried about keeping their job or working harder to prove to their boss how indispensable they were.

This had gotten even worse since the power company started dismissing people for no apparent reason. Almost half the town had been employed at the power plant, including George's dad, but five years ago the power company's managing director began firing any employee he wanted to for any reason he could think of.

George knew, in fact everybody knew, that the managing director was called Mr Watt. He might have been quite muscular when he was younger but now he had spent the last three decades eating so many pork pies and chocolate cake that his belly had ballooned to the size of a football.

Every day he wore the same muddy brown coloured suit, with big wide lapels and big bell-bottom flares and he always wore with it a blue spotty tie. Mr Watt looked permanently angry, but most men who have lost all the hair on top of their heads feel bitter about it, so they grow their hair long at one side and swoop it over, pretending to cover up the bald bit over the top.

And of course, angry Mr Watt the power plant managing director was married to evil old Mrs Watt, the mental marker throwing teacher. George thought they were well suited together.

At first, Mr Watt started firing people just for being late, even once. After that, he fired people who took too long at the toilet. Then he fired people for not taking long enough in the toilet because he thought they weren't washing their hands properly. It was rumoured that Mr. Watt had become a bit of a cleanliness freak with an obsession that was bordering on a compulsion. Now even George knew that everybody should wash their hands after they've been to the toilet but only Mr. Watt could go to the toilet with rubber gloves on, in case he touched the same door handle or tap as someone who hadn't washed their hands properly. He even fired people who left a bit of a smell in the toilet after they'd done a number two.

But the worst crime of all, up at 3P's Power plant, was if Mr. Watt caught anyone picking their nose. Mr. Watt would fire the nauseating nose-picker, with immediate effect, with no wages and no reference.

Mr. Watt was a nasty man and an even nastier boss.

So up until five years ago, Mr. Watt ruled the power plant with fear and iron control and everybody was scared of him. Nobody enjoyed coming to work any more as Mr. Watt forced all his employees to work harder in his drive to make his power plant the most effective and profitable power plant in the world. That was when George's dad lost his job.

George's dad had been fired for being late on a Monday morning but was allowed to work until Friday, when he could collect his final wage. When Friday came, George's dad was standing outside the managing director's office waiting to sign for his final pay packet when he decided he would deliver a final act of vengeance toward Mr Watt so George's dad decided to pick his nose (his own nose, not Mr. Watt's).

It was a really good nostril scratcher too, one that dragged out a crispy bit of bogey stuck together with a snotty bit of gunge and a little bit of dried blood too. George's dad rubbed the bogey into his hands and walked into Mr. Watt's office, picked up Mr. Watt's favourite pen and signed for his wages, gumming up the gold shaft of the pen with snot. Finally, George's dad shook Mr. Watt's hand firmly and thanked him for allowing him to work at the plant for so long. Mr. Watt couldn't understand why, even when he was being sacked, George's dad was leaving his office smiling broadly. It was only after George's dad had left the office did Mr Watt notice the green, crusty mucus crushed into his hand. Then Mr Watt decided to stop shaking hands and start wearing rubber surgical gloves.

Everybody knew that the power plant was officially called 3P's Power after the founders but now the workers had secretly started calling the power company the 3P's after the Pickers, the Pee-ers and the Poopers, after the three favourite reasons Mr. Watt had for firing people.

But this didn't make anyone in the town any happier and people just became more and more miserable. Mr Watt had fired almost everyone at the power station. Unemployment was high in Little Pumpington where the power station had once provided so many jobs, even if nobody actually liked working there but at least it was a wage. The people of Little Pumpington were bitter and felt sorry for themselves. Nobody really cared about anybody else in the town and George was right; it had been getting worse for years.

V. THE BIG BROWN BAG OF POO PRANK

George left the school an hour after everybody else. Detention sucked!

Mrs Watt had made George clean every interactive white board in every class and computer room in the whole school and his wrists now ached from all the scrubbing. At the end of one of the most eventful school-days George could remember, he walked out of the schools gates, pondering over his 'debates' with Mrs Watt, both real and imaginary, his pen-inflicted head wounds and the fact absolutely no one in school seemed to be worried about Old Mr Swan's disappearance.

'He hasn't disappeared,' the other boys said to George in the playground at break-time, 'he's gone off on holiday.'

'But don't you think his sudden departure's a bit strange?' argued George.

'No, potato head!' shouted the boys and they kept on playing football until the bell rang.

Allison was standing, waiting for him at the school gates.

'Hi!' she said.

'Hi yourself.' muttered George.

'I went home to tell my mum I was going to wait for you, since it was kinda my fault you got into trouble today.' Allison sympathised. George didn't reply. 'You're not still mad with that old bat, are you?' asked Allison. 'Don't let her get to you. Chill out, have fun.' oozed the girl enthusiastically.

'I will be having fun when I get away from this dump,' moaned George, 'I'm going round to my Grandpa Jock's house and he's brilliant fun.'

'Ooh, that sounds good, can I come?'

'No,' shouted George, 'you haven't asked your mum and erm, anyway, erm, my grandpa doesn't like girls around since girls don't like the games that boys play.'

'I do so, and I'll prove it to you.' said Allison running off, around the corner and by the time George reached the end of the road, Allison was standing there, waiting patiently in her jeans and sweatshirt.

'My mum says it's OK if I go round to your Grandpa's house with you and I can get as dirty as I want because I'm wearing my old jeans so I can play boys games if I want to.' Allison said without pausing for breath and reluctantly George led the way, passed Allison's house, round the corner and into the cul-de-sac directly opposite.

Away to the end of the cul-de-sac was a small wooden glade, a grassy clump where a handful of trees stood and a large tree trunk lay on the ground. The trunk was old and cracked and the grass had been scraped bare around it. Any dry twigs and dead branches on the trunk had been worn clean over the years by a thousand small feet. George used to play there when he was younger and the tree trunk had been a car, a pirate ship, a space rocket and even the occasional horse. And just before this grassy knoll, in the corner at the end of the road, was where Grandpa Jock lived.

As they approached the little house, they began to hear a funny sound.

Eeeeoowwwweeeyyeeeeooohhhheeeyyyooooowwwww wwwwwwww!

'What is that hideous noise?' screamed Allison, putting her hands over her ears and trying to block out the screeching. George just smiled.

'It sounds like a cat is being tortured. It's horrible.' cried Allison, trying to make herself heard above the droning, whining racket.

'Yes, yes, that's it. It's a cat, in pain. Maybe you should just go home, it's not the kind of thing you'd want to hear.' insisted George a little too eagerly.

'No, I'm staying,' insisted Allison, 'you won't get rid of me that easily, George.'

The shrieking, squealing din continued and even started to get louder as George and Allison walked through Grandpa Jock's gate and round to his back door. The air seemed to be trembling and the flowers in the plant-pots were shaking; even the garden gnome with the little red hat was bouncing and his fishing rod was waving up and down. The noise began to become unbearable and Allison felt the noise rumble in her tummy now.

But just as soon as it had started, the noise stopped screeching and slowly droned to a silence. There was a man standing in the doorway, holding what looked like tartan octopus with very stiff legs.

'Who's this then?' shouted Grandpa Jock excitedly.

'What's that then?' shrieked Allison in amazement.

'Grandpa, this is Allison, she's the new girl at school,' said George, 'and Allison, these are my Grandpa Jock's bagpipes.'

'Bagpipes! Wow, I've never seen bagpipes before.' uttered Allison wide-eyed. 'But do they always make that awful noise.'

'Not at all, lassie,' said Grandpa Jock indignantly, 'I was jist gettin' warmed up. Listen.'

And Grandpa Jock slung three of the 'legs' over his shoulder, grasped one leg with his fingers delicately and put the other one in his mouth and started to blow.

'That's the chanter.' whispered George, pointing to where Grandpa Jock's fingers were resting. The droning started as Grandpa Jock blew hard into the tartan bag and it filled with hot air. Then he gently squeezed with his elbow and the 'cat' started screeching again.

Eeeeoowwwweeeyyeeeeoooohhhheeeyyyooooowwwww
wwwwwwww!

Allison put her hands over her ears as she was deafened
by the vibrating wall of noise and her tummy began to
rumble inside again.

Then, as Grandpa Jock's fingers began to dance across the
holes on his chanter, Allison was amazed to hear music in
her ears; a tune which she barely recognised had her
nodding her head to the rhythm and the sing-song
squealing with the secondary droning sound reaching
inside her chest, grabbing her stomach and wobbling it
around. This wasn't just music to her ears; this was music
for her whole body.

With a triumphant 'taa-daaa' at the end, Grandpa Jock
finger's stopped dancing, he dropped the mouthplece
from his lips and bowed to accept the applause from
George and Allison. As he bowed forward, one of the
three longer droning pipes on his shoulder dropped down
and bonked George on the head.

'Oops, sorry lad.' said Grandpa Jock.

'That's OK, Grandpa.' replied George. Grandpa Jock did
seem much more excited than usual today.

'That was brilliant!' exclaimed Allison in amazement.

'Well, thank you, young lady,' and Grandpa Jock bowed graciously, 'I love playing my bagpipes and I love listening to the music of a band of pipe and drums.'

'Grandpa Jock used to be a sergeant major in a pipe band.' said George proudly.

'I've got all my favourite music on this 'ere I-Pod nano thingamajig,' said Grandpa Jock, pulling out a thin white disk and two earpieces on thin white wires.

'You've got an I-Pod?' shrieked Allison, 'But you're ancient, er, I mean, sorry, you're old, I mean......' and Allison stopped before she put both her feet in it.

'That's alright, lassie,' smiled Grandpa Jock, 'I'm seventy four years old and just because someone's old, doesn't mean they can't stop learning. Look!' And from inside his shirt, beneath his vest, he pulled out a shiny, little black stick which hung on a piece of cord.

'See, my USB doo-dah stick thing!' said Grandpa proudly as he waved the little memory capsule around. 'I'm so up with technology I keep all my favourite tunes aroon' my neck all the time. That way I can play it in the car or anywhere.'

Allison was impressed and George was impressed that Allison was impressed. George began to think he'd been wrong about her.

'And what's that one?' asked Allison pointing to a small blue gadget on the same cord.

'That's my emergency bagpipe repair kit, that is,' replied Grandpa Jock quickly. 'It's brand new.' And one at a time he popped up a small screwdriver, followed by a tiny pair of scissors and finally a miniature nail file.

'Well, not everybody likes the sound of the bagpipes, you know, especially around here.' Grandpa Jock went on.

'What do you mean?' asked Allison, puzzled.

'Put it this way,' said Grandpa Jock with a gleam in his eye, 'what's the difference between an onion and the bagpipes?'

'We don't know.' yelled George and Allison together.

'Nobody cries when you chop up the bagpipes!' And Grandpa Jock burst out laughing at his own joke. When he got his breath back, he turned to George and said, 'And it's about time you brought one of your little friends round, lad.'

George was about to speak when he noticed Allison staring at Grandpa Jock, with her mouth open. Now that he'd stopped playing his bagpipes, Allison could see Grandpa Jock properly and she was having a good look.

Grandpa Jock was a tall, thin man and his face was long and slim, like a horse's but he had red cheeks and his nose was big, plump and purple as if it wasn't made for his face. Even the little dangly bits at the bottom of Grandpa Jock's ears were purple. He had no hair on the top of his head but he made up for that with lots of gingery hair around the back and the sides. This would stick out in all directions, particularly after Grandpa Jock had been having his afternoon nap or he'd been blowing hard into his bagpipes. In fact, the harder he blew, the more his hair would stick up.

As Allison stared, George realised what she was thinking, 'Maybe I get my gorgeous looks from my Grandpa Jock, then?' George said, with a rueful smile.

'Aye, lass. There's plenty o' character in this face, an'a.' said Grandpa Jock in a very broad Scottish accent and he burst out laughing again. George joined in and soon Allison was laughing too, even though she couldn't quite understand what Grandpa Jock was saying.

'So tell me whit ye's did at school today.' asked Grandpa Jock and George told him all about his new desk buddy, his marker pen wounds, the speed of light debate and detention.

'Aye, she's a mad yin, that.' agreed Grandpa Jock and a twinkle began to show itself beneath his bushy eyebrows. 'Should we let young Allison into oor gang?' he whispered.

'Well, she is kinda cool, Grandpa,' said George shyly, 'she does like your bagpipes and she did call Mrs Watt a stuck-up dragon within five minutes of coming into our class.'

'That's good enough for me, boy,' laughed Grandpa Jock heartily, 'I've been thinking o' ways to move oor mischief up to new record levels. And today seems to be the day. We'll get him and her, at the same time.'

'Why both of them?' asked George puzzled.

'Finally, lad,' winked Grandpa Jock, 'It's payback time, and I'm going to enjoy this so much.'

Now Grandpa Jock loved playing games and always had time for fun and mischief.

His favourite games usually involved picking on Mr. Watt, perhaps for sacking George's dad, perhaps because it was fun but maybe there was something else. After school some days, George and Grandpa Jock would to creep round to Mr. Watt's house, ring his doorbell and run away.

Mr. Watt would come to the front door and look around quizzically to see who'd rang his bell, then realizing he'd been tricked he would storm back into his house, muttering to himself.

Not far away, hiding in the big bushes in the garden of the corner house would be George and Grandpa Jock, breathlessly holding their sides with laughter and pointing to Mr. Watt's house, before falling about again in fits of giggles.

And it was always a race between George and Grandpa Jock to see who could annoy Mr. Watt the most, raising the managing director's blood pressure with ever more ludicrous rings of his front door bell until the winner was decided when Mr. Watt would shout random furies to an empty street.

Of course, the more adventurous the ring, the less time the ringer had to run into hiding, and often, Grandpa Jock was almost caught after ringing the doorbell six or seven times. George, on the other hand was never caught. Not because he didn't ring Mr. Watt's bell in a particularly adventurous way, he did, but George was always a much faster runner than Grandpa Jock, whose knees creaked and cracked with even the slightest bit of exercise.

'I'm not as fit as I used to be, lad,' Grandpa Jock would wheeze. 'I'm eighty two, you know.'

'But I thought you...never mind, Grandpa.' And George stopped himself from saying what he was thinking.

Not that Mr. Watt could have caught them if he tried to run after them. Mr. Watt's big belly was way too fat to be carried around, giving chase to anyone. In fact, George often thought, that because Mr. Watt's tummy was so big and round, that it wasn't really his tummy but a football that he'd shoved up his shirt. When George was younger, he often imagined Mr. Watt was a huge football fan and at lunchtime, he'd walk into his factory floor and shout, 'Who's for a game of footie, then lads?' and pull the ball out from under his shirt and start a kick about.

But then Mr. Watt fired George's dad and George realised that Mr. Watt was just a big, fat meanie and his belly was real after all.

Although, quite why Grandpa Jock disliked Mr. Watt so much or why Mr. Watt was always at home in the afternoon when, as the managing director of a massive power plant, he should really be sitting in his office, was never quite clear to George. What was clear was that Grandpa Jock really didn't like Mr. Watt at all and hadn't done so for many years. Grandpa Jock always said that whatever they did to Mr. Watt would never be enough to repay him for what he'd done to the town.

'He's bleeding us dry.' Grandpa Jock would say but not actually reveal any more.

'What do you mean, Grandpa?' George would urge.

'Never mind, son. No-one would believe you anyway,' Grandpa Jock would always conclude.

Today though, Grandpa Jock had been brewing over a big new prank and now that Allison had joined them, it made this mischief even more exciting. Grandpa Jock ran outside to his garden, returned two seconds later and jumped into the kitchen. He was holding a small, red plastic spade that George used to take to the beach, and waving around a brown paper bag, whilst rummaging in the kitchen drawer.

'Ah, found them,' Grandpa Jock proclaimed as he pulled from the drawer a large box of safety matches. He rattled the box.

'Don't try this at home, kids,' laughed Grandpa Jock., 'do it roond at your grandpa's house; he'll let you do anything!'

'Noo, quick, let's go,' he whispered, looking around secretively, 'before your mother comes round and catches us.'

'Where are we going, Grandpa?' asked George, puzzled as they walked around the corner and towards Mr. Watts house.

'This is it, my boy. This is the big one.' joked Grandpa Jock excitedly. 'This is when we truly get our own back on that Mr. Watt and all his nonsense and his mad teacher wife too. This, my gruesome twosome, is what I call 'The Big Brown Bag of Poo Prank.''

'The Big Brown Bag of Poo Prank?' George and Allison said together.

'What's that, Grandpa?' said George, intrigued.

'Yes, lad, this is the ultimate. This will put us in the history books. Watch and learn.' And off Grandpa Jock ran down the street and round the corner until he reached the edge of Mr. Watt's garden. He waved to George to hide in their usual hiding place in the bushes then he crept over onto Mr. Watt's lawn with the brown paper bag out in from of him.

From the edge of the neighbouring garden, George and Allison saw the object of Grandpa Jock's attentions. It was a large, dark brown pile of dog poo. The people of Little Pumpington were very horrible and would usually let dogs' poo anywhere, even on, especially on, Mr Watt's lawn.

The big dog's doo-dah looked fresh and George would swear that he could still see steam rising from it. Allison reckoned that the dog who'd laid it must have been very large indeed. But why was Grandpa Jock helping Mr. Watt clean up the mess from his grass? George thought. Grandpa Jock took out the little red spade, gently scooped up the doggy doo and popped it into the brown paper bag. Then he carefully rolled up the end of the bag into a nice little parcel.

After that, the stealthy old man sneaked off the grass, onto the driveway, across the stones and onto the porch. He carefully laid the bag on the tiles on the floor, reached into his pocket and brought out the large box of matches.

Grandpa Jock then took one match out of the box and struck it against the rough edge.

George and Allison watched in amazement as the match flared brightly then flickered slowly into an orange flame. Grandpa Jock held the light closely to the edge of the bag. Wisps of smoke began to rise from the corner of the paper.

Seconds later the bag was beginning to show long, thin fingers of flame rising from the top. Black smoke began to pour out and the flames began to reach higher and higher. Soon the whole bag was ablaze and Grandpa Jock stretched to his feet, stepped to the side next to the bell and held his finger on the button for one long continuous ringgggggggggggggggggggg.

Then he was off, running as fast as his seventy four year old legs or eighty two year old legs (whichever you believed) could carry him, his strides were short and tight and his legs looked like they were being snapped back together with invisible elastic bands. Grandpa Jock jumped the small wall at the bottom of the garden, ran across the road without looking, which you should never do, and dived into the bushes beside George and Allison, puffing and panting like an old dog.

Then... nothing. George peaked out from behind his thick clump of bushes. The bag was now burning furiously and black wisps of paper were beginning to float up into the sky.

Finally, Mr. Watt answered the door. He opened it slowly at first, thinking this was another trick and then threw open the door when he saw the burning parcel. With a burst of speed never before seen by someone so fat, he leapt on the blazing bag, stamping out the flames with his slippered feet.

Squidge, squidge, squidge.

On the fifth or sixth stamp, Mr. Watt slowed his stamps down, realizing that the contents of the bag were very squishy and not terribly pleasant.

He leaned against the door with one hand and held his ankle up with other, inspecting the sole of his blue suede slippers, with his bursting belly hanging over the top of his trousers. Then, with a wild shake of his fist, Mr. Watt began screaming at no-one in particular and he ran out onto the grass. Still shouting, he dragged the sole of his slipper over the lawn, trying to scrape off the poo.

Grandpa Jock, Allison and George were now having great difficulty stifling their laughter, their sides were about to burst, Grandpa Jock's face was even redder than before and his nose definitely looking as if it would explode. Tears streamed down all their faces as they fought to contain their mirth. Slowly, just when their fits of laughter began to subside, all it took was for them to look each other in the eyes before Grandpa quietly spluttered...

'B-b-bag of poo!' and that set them all off again, uncontrollably sniggering and snorting in the bushes.

Peeking out, they watched Mr. Watt limp back into his house before another voice joined the commotion. It was Mrs Watt, their psychopathic pen-throwing teacher!

She was usually at school when Grandpa Jock and George pulled their usual stunts against Mr Watt but they were later today because George had been in detention so Mrs Watt was home.

'Get out of this house with that muck on your feet!' screeched the wild haired teacher in her dressing gown. Mrs. Petunia Watt (formerly Prickly) certainly let herself go when she wasn't in school and looked nothing like the prim and proper school mistress now.

She was clearly unimpressed with the mess that Mr. Watt had been dragging onto the carpet and was now pushing him out of the door and back onto the grass. In her rush to get her filthy footed husband out of the house, Mrs. Watt stepped on the now smouldering bag. The bag, greasy with burnt poo, slid across the porch and Mrs. Watt plopped down onto the floor, landing onto her skinny bottom. Realising what she was sitting in, Mrs. Watt burst into tears and the poo-footed Mr. Watt helped his now smelly-bottomed wife into the house, leaving his ruined slippers lying on the steps and taking one final look up and down the street, before locking the front door.

It took Allison, George and Grandpa Jock fifteen minutes to stop laughing and begin to calm down. Only then was it safe for them to sneak out of their hide-out and stagger off home.

'You were right, George,' said Allison, 'your Grandpa is great fun.'

'That was a beauty,' chuckled Grandpa Jock, 'but we'd best keep oor heids doon fur a bit.'

'What did he say?' asked Allison, puzzled.

'He said we'd better keep our heads down, you know, stay out of trouble for a few days.' replied George as they walked passed Allison's house.

'See you tomorrow.' Allison said as she waved to the other two.

'Yeah, cool. See you in the morning.' smiled George as he waved back and before long George and his Grandpa had walked back to George's house, where his mum and dad had returned from work and were in the kitchen making dinner.

'Thanks Grandpa. That was great fun tonight.' giggled George as he said goodbye.

'Well, you be careful, boy. That kinda stuff has ways of finding you out and biting yer bum.' warned Grandpa Jock, mischievously smiling.

That night Grandpa Jock vanished.

VI. MR WATT AND THE OLD PEOPLE

Five years ago, Mr. Watt had thought very hard about how to get more people to use more energy. Being 'environmentally friendly' was not on Mr. Watt's agenda, he just wanted people to burn more electricity, racking up bigger bills in the process and creating more profit for his power company.

Mr. Watt became angry when he thought about people not staying in their houses. When people stayed in their warm cosy houses, they used more electricity, they kept their central heating on all day and their televisions were switched on all the time, even when there was no-one in the room to watch it.

Lights were left blazing and kettles were boiled regularly throughout the day whenever people fancied a cup of tea. People couldn't do that if they were up the town, shopping, paying bills or posting parcels at the post office.

Mr. Watt had realised that shops would always keep their lights and their heating on when they were open and switch them off when they closed. Shops, supermarkets and shopping centres would always burn the same amount of electricity regardless of how many or how few shoppers there were.

The only time Mr. Watt thought he couldn't control people's power consumption was when they weren't in their own homes so he had to think of ways to keep people inside their houses for longer.

Of course, people still had to go out now and again so Mr. Watt thought of ways to get people back into their houses quicker. Making people miserable and scared was just a bonus when compared to his master plan. Miserable and scared people didn't want to go outside to visit their friends so people didn't get together to share the same heating and electricity. They stayed in their own houses, using double or treble the power than if they were all together, having fun and sharing their company as well as the heating.

Mr. Watt realised that the people who used the lowest amount of electricity were old people. Old people were very frugal and didn't like wasting money. Even in the worst of winters, old people were reluctant to switch on their heating too much. Instead they'd rather 'put on another cardigan.'

Old people often watched television but when they did so they usually turned the lights off so they could see the picture clearer. When they switched the TV off, only then did they switch their lights on; or not lights, usually just one light.

Old people did boil their kettles frequently because old people loved drinking cups of tea but since they weren't as strong as they used to be, they'd usually just boil enough water in the kettle for one or two cups so that it was easier and lighter for them to pick the kettle up.

Younger people filled their kettles full of water in the morning and then boiled that same water again and again, every time they wanted a cup of tea or coffee. This wasted so much electricity since the water was left to go cold in the kettle then boiled later for another cuppa.

But it was five years ago that Mr. Watt had his greatest revelation. He was standing in the queue at the bank, waiting to pay a large bag of money into the power company's account. (Mr. Watt didn't trust anybody else to do it) and it was at this point that he realised in the two queues in front of him were seven people, two of them were students, one man who Mr Watt thought didn't have a job, two ladies with young children, and then two old people. Mr Watt joined the shortest queue.

Mr. Watt really didn't like old people. They didn't use enough electricity and he thought that they smelled of wee and cold cabbage.

'And what are old people doing in the bank anyway?' thought Mr. Watt, 'They are not supposed to have any money.' He muttered to himself, wrinkling his nose up.

There were two counters open at the bank and the queue seemed to be taking a long time, moving in fits and starts. Then Mr. Watt noticed that the student walked up to one window quickly, asked a question, paid his money across, and took his receipt and left, quite promptly.

'Bish, bash, bosh, nice and quick,' thought Mr Watt, 'now, go home and turn your computer on.'

Next, the young mother managed to wheel her pram up to the counter quite quickly, sign her withdrawal slip, take her cash and moved away within 90 seconds.

'Come on, quicker now.' muttered Mr Watt, 'Home you go, turn on the heating full blast.'

Then the whole process slowed right down. Instead of moving to the window as soon as the young mother had moved away, the old lady waited patiently in line until the teller called her across. Then she shuffled slowly and carefully up to the counter, placed her bag on the shelf and began to rummage around at the bottom of it.

'Why didn't you do that when you were standing in the queue?' hissed Mr Watt.

Eventually, she found her little money bag and began writing out her deposit slip, chatting away to the teller all the time.

'Come on, come on. Hurry up!' mumbled Mr. Watt and he swore under his breath, 'We haven't got all day.' He was beginning to hop from one foot to the other in a very agitated fashion, working himself into a tiny, self-contained frenzy.

By the time the people in the other queue, the second student, the job-dodging layabout (Mr Watt had decided to call him) and the other young mum had been served promptly, the other old person had now reached their counter and was taking an eternity. Finally, the old customer at the front of his queue had been served and it was Mr. Watt's turn to approach the counter. He almost kicked the old lady out of the way in his impatient rage.

'About time too,' he growled at the bank clerk, 'don't these smelly old people realise that some of us have jobs to do. They should stay in their houses and not get in the way of normal, everyday life.'

'Oh no,' smiled the bank clerk politely, 'It makes their day to get out and chat. Sometimes old people don't have anyone else to talk too. I think it's sweet.'

Well, Mr. Watt didn't think it was sweet, as he walked out of the bank. He thought it was a nuisance, a hindrance and a blooming big frustration.

Outside the bank, Mr Watt stopped. He looked out across the High Street and he saw that there were old people everywhere. Lots of old men, and even more old ladies. All of them just shuffling between shops, or sometimes sitting inside little cafés, eating tea and cakes or clogging up the High St and getting in people's way by pulling their trolley bags behind them.

Then Mr. Watt looked in through the shop windows. In almost every shop, at the front of every queue, there was an old person, taking their time and having a nice chat with the shop assistant. Mr. Watt could see the other people waiting in line and they were as impatient and frustrated as he had been in the bank.

'These people have places to go!' thought Mr. Watt. 'Those oldies are stopping other people from using more of my electricity.'

So not only were old people not using their own electricity, they were slowing down everyone else, stopping them from getting back home to switch the lights, turn the TV on and turn the central heating right up.

Still festering, Mr Watt continued to walk down the street until something caught his eye. He stopped at a shop window and stared in. It was the pet shop and on display, in the middle, was a stack of cages, one on top of another. In each cage was a fat, little hamster. There was also a wheel in every cage and as Mr Watt watched, the hamsters would continually jump into their wheel, run as fast as their stubby legs could carry them for a few minutes and then jump off again.

Inside Mr. Watt's head, a gigantic light bulb appeared. The idea that lit up his imagination had conjured a huge, glowing orb of heat powered by Mr Watt's brainwave. But

Mr Watt's idea wasn't about saving energy. His light bulb idea wasn't energy efficient. His big bulb was burning off heat, not light, wasting energy, and this thought always made Mr. Watt very happy.

He suddenly knew what the 3P's Power Company had to do to make almost limitless amounts of energy and obscene amounts of profit. Mr. Watt then put his grand plan in to action.

VII. THE GRAND PLAN... ALMOST

Part of this grand plan was to make the people of Little Pumpington more and more miserable each year. Mr Watt began deliberately making people depressed and worse than that, the 3P's Power Company were even encouraging people to be horrible to each other.

Posters and advertising billboards started appearing around the town four or five years ago with a very strange slogan on them.

'They may be smelly, they may be old. Geriatrics should be sold!'

George first saw one of these adverts when he was out shopping with his mum and dad.

'What's a geri-atric?' he asked, slightly bemused.

'It's when Jurgen Klinnsman scored three goals for Spurs at football.' said George's dad and he started laughing to himself again. 'Back page of the Sun! Classic! Heh heh heh.' Dad sniggered but George just shook his head.

'Never mind your father,' tutted George's mum, giving dad a look of disgust, 'a geriatric is another word for an old person.' she said impatiently.

People were now laughing at these slogans all over town and the more people laughed at them, the crueller the slogans became:

'Electricity would be free, if old people didn't smell of wee' said one of the posters.

'Life's a drag cos of all the old codgers. Don't wait in line for the coffin dodgers' announced the next one.

Drivers would blare their horns at poor old people when they were crossing the road. Some men and women in queues would even push old people out of the way in shops and barge past them on the pavement.

Horrible people would actually whisper to old people 'You should be sold' or 'You smell of wee' and of course, old people had way too much dignity to reply.

After months of these posters being all over town, they were replaced by another set of adverts, even more ghastly than before and as the people of Little Pumpington were becoming crueller and nastier, more people thought these slogans were even funnier and soon they were all laughing together in a horrid sort of way.

'Their pensions are paid out from your wages, but they stand in shops just taking ages' proclaimed the next poster.

'Everyone else is faster and slicker. Dump the old duffers and life would be quicker!' read the second poster, becoming ruder.

'They're all just old, wrinkly and grey. Life would be better if they all went away!'

The third poster seemed to be prophesising a change was coming to the town. And very soon, for some strange, unknown reason, there were less and less old people around the town. Maybe they didn't want to go out any more, or maybe they didn't want to be the butt of the town's big joke. Nobody really noticed though as more nasty posters were put up on billboards.

But queues did move faster to begin with, there were fewer pensioners blocking the pavements and real customers could visit all the shops, the bank and the post office and still be home in time to put the kettle on, turn on the TV and crank up the central heating for a cosy night in by the fire.

Occasionally, very, very occasionally, neighbours would drop in to check on the old person who lived next door. Maybe they hadn't seen their old neighbour for a few days and although they didn't really care too much about them, their conscience would be pricked and they'd stick their head around the door.

Usually, the old codgers' front door was unlocked but there was never anyone at home. Almost always, there was a little note on the table or stuck on the fridge with a magnet that said,

'Gone to visit Aunty Flo, be home soon.'

Or

'Fed up with those blooming adverts. Gone to live in Florida.'

Everyone in the town assumed that most of the old people had just nipped off to visit their friends or family or had emigrated to another country. No-one really stopped to think why or how, or even if the old people had gone, why they had left their houses unlocked and why they hadn't taken all their belongings with them.

All people were interested in was getting round the shops quickly, getting home from their work and staying in their houses all night, watching TV with all the lights on and burning their central heating full blast. This, of course meant their electricity bills went up too.

After a while, slowly, so slowly in fact that no-one noticed, the queues in the shops started to get longer again. Because there were fewer old people around, shops didn't need as many shop assistants, banks didn't need to have two counters open, they only needed one counter open and one bank clerk working behind it. This poor bank clerk usually had to work harder than ever just to keep up. As shops and banks and post offices cut back on their staff, more people lost their jobs, then queues became longer, everybody got grumpier and nobody noticed that there were fewer old people around or that life hadn't really gotten much better at all.

Life had probably gotten worse but the town's people were all too obsessed with looking after themselves and looking after their jobs to care too much about other people so the grind of daily life in the town went on. Everyone had to work harder and everyone became poorer as the cost of power went up and up. Almost certainly, no-one was any happier.

Except Mr. Watt. In the last five years, the 3P's Power Company had recorded bigger and bigger profits. Each years sales were higher than the last as people spent more time in their houses, using his valuable electricity.

But more than that, the cost of running the power plant had declined. Mr. Watt boasted to the other power company directors that he had introduced a unique new way of generating power without using any more coal or oil to burn in the furnaces. This cut costs at the plant, making the company's profits even bigger and Mr. Watt was given a special award for this environmentally friendly carbon reductions scheme.

Mr. Watt had made such a song and dance about his top secret, power saving, environmentally friendly technology that he persuaded the Mayor of Little Pumpington to host a huge gala award ceremony in his honour.

Everybody who was anybody in the town was invited, as well as every school, since the Mayor thought that Mr. Watt would set a terrific example to all the children, encouraging them to be even more environmentally friendly. But most children know that they are much 'greener' than their parents are, because grown-ups never realise what's good for them, until it's too late.

VIII. MR WATT'S PRESENTATION

The next morning George had woken early, scoffed his toast quickly before it could get lost inside his jacket and set off for school to find Allison, still quietly laughing at the big brown bag of poo prank. His dad hadn't returned from his walk yet but that wasn't unusual as he said he was dropping into Grandpa Jock's house. And at this point, no one knew Grandpa Jock had disappeared.

Allison was waiting for George at the end of the road. 'That was great fun yesterday,' she said, 'but aren't you a little bit scared that Mrs Watt saw us?'

'No, we've never been seen before in those bushes and there are so many places to hide in Mrs Watt's street that she'd never know where to look.' replied George grinning.

The morning passed uneventfully, with George on his best behaviour, except occasionally when a big grin broke out across his face when he thought about Mrs Watt sliding about in the bag of poo on her doorstep. Mrs Watt seemed to be oblivious to George's enjoyment.

Just before lunch, Mrs Watt stood before the class and announced, 'This afternoon we will all be going to the town hall for an environmental presentation. Please line up in the playground at one o'clock sharp for the bus.'

George had forgotten all about this school trip. His mum had signed his permission slip two weeks ago and with all the adventure in the last couple of days, he'd completely forgotten about it. And for George, although visiting the boring old town hall wasn't his idea of a great school trip, this was a good excuse to get out of the class for the afternoon.

As the bus pulled out of the playground and along the main road, George sat at the front besides Allison and looked out of the window. Up ahead, looming above the town at the top of the hill, they saw the power plant with its three tall thin chimneys standing redundant, no longer belching out filthy black smoke as they once had, and the rest of the buildings shimmering like a polished, stainless steel castle.

'Why is the power station so shiny?' asked Allison, who'd only lived in the town less than a week.

'I dunno,' replied George carelessly, 'I think it's something to do with the company's new cleaner power but nobody knows much about it. At least, that's what my dad says.'

Just along from the school, to the right, Allison and George saw the latest poster produced by the power company, as part of their campaign to force people to use more electricity. Since there were fewer old people around these days, Mr. Watt had turned his attention to children, specifically trying to scare little kids. Some of George's classmates had said that their little brothers and sisters had had nightmares after seeing the terrifying posters that the 3P's Power Company had put up all over town.

This first poster that caught George's eye was a picture of a purple and black, grizzly monster, gnashing his ginormous teeth which were dripping with blood. The caption underneath the creature said,

'This ugly creature lives under your bed. Keep your light on or he'll bite off your head!'

As the bus drove on, George saw a second poster, on a large billboard next to the nursery school. It showed a giant spider dangling down from the ceiling, with eight hairy legs reaching out to snatch a very scared little boy, who was hiding under the duvet. This time the slogan was

'So scared that you might wet the bed? Just keep your bedroom light on instead.'

In fact, as George looked closer at the poster, he saw that it showed splashes of wee, dribbling from the bottom of the little boy's bed. 'Way too much information.' thought George.

Just before the school bus arrived at the town hall, George spotted another poster, this time outside the town's burger bar. George thought about this for a moment and realised that after the school and nursery, the burger bar was the place where it was absolutely certain that children would always go. George didn't like burgers too much, he always thought that they tasted a bit like grease and sawdust (not that George had ever tasted sawdust before) but he couldn't understand why people would want to shovel them into their mouths every day.

KEEP YOUR BEDROOM LIGHT ON FOR AS LONG AS YOU CAN, OR ELSE YOU'LL BE DINNER FOR THE BOGEYMAN

George also thought that it was rather sneaky of the power company to put these scary posters up on big billboards in exactly the places where children would see them, probably scaring the little kids half out of their minds.

This time the poster showed a scaly green arm, matted with black hair and long fingers that were tipped with dirty fingernails, stretching out from underneath a bed and reaching round to grab the terrified, blonde-haired little girl, who was crying. The caption at the bottom was written in red ink, which George guessed that this was meant to be blood, as it appeared to dripping from the bottom of the letters. It read,

'Keep your bedroom light on for as long as you can, Or else you'll be dinner for the Bogeyman!'

George actually thought the posters were quite cool but he could see how they might scare really young children. 'I can understand why Grandpa Jock really hates the Mr. Watt.' thought George as the bus pulled up in front of the town hall.

All the children piled out of the bus, walked through the large front doors and into the auditorium, where the award ceremony was being held. Above the door was a large white banner that proclaimed, 'The Society of Future Achievers'.

Mrs Watt made George sit at the very front, next to her, so she could keep an eye on him and Allison chose the seat next to George since no one else wanted to sit that close to Mrs Watt.

George looked along the row and saw all the other members of the Future Achievers Society sitting in their grey suits, with white shirts and plain ties. All of the buttons on their white cotton shirts seemed to be straining against the large bulging bellies. The starchy white material was stretched tightly against their tummies and it was clear that these men enjoyed long lunches and far too much beer. Their round faces were bright red and their cheeks were puffed out as they waited for the ceremony to begin. Mr. Watt sat in the middle of the front row.

'These fat old men don't look like future achievers,' whispered Allison to George. 'they look like they've done all their achieving and now don't want anyone else to join their club.'

Before long, the mayor walked on to the stage, wearing his usual red cloak, trimmed with white and black spotted fur and wearing the biggest gold chain George had ever seen. In his hand, he carried a little silver trophy in the shape of a chimney stack. George presumed that this was meant to look like one of the three large chimneys up at the power plant but since this award was supposed to be for being environmentally friendly, George thought the idea was a pretty stupid one.

The mayor called Mr. Watt up onto the stage and proceeded to tell the audience all about the Society of Future Achievers. It turns out that all the directors across the country had decided to get together to form their own power plant owners association, giving themselves the very grand sounding title of The Society of Future Achievers. To George it seemed that the Future Achievers had only formed their own little club and every now and then, they awarded themselves prizes for no other reason than to make themselves feel more important, more stuck up and more pompous.

Then followed a promotional film about the success of the 3P's Power plant that told everyone in the audience absolutely nothing about Mr. Watt's miracle new technology but instead showed pictures of children chasing little bunny rabbits across flower-covered meadows. There were many pictures of the outside of the power plant but none from the inside. There were old black and white photographs of the power plant's founders, Mr. Peabody, Mr. Percival and Mr. Prickly followed by cheesy publicity photographs of a smug Mr. Watt giving the big thumbs-up to the camera from different angles whilst captions went whizzing by at the bottom of the video.

'Cleaner, Greener and Meaner than ever before!' read the words as they flew across the giant screen from right to left. 'Believe it. One day all this will be yours!' they announced, somewhat mystically. All the time, the sneering Mr. Watt was looking smugger and smugger in his own self-proclaiming commercial.

And he did actually have a lot to be smug about. The other directors in the Society of Future Achievers were incredibly jealous of Mr. Watt's new technology and they would have done anything to steal it for themselves but evil Mr. Watt kept his trade secrets very closely guarded. Throughout the film, he stood on the stage, grinning

'Congratulations, Mr. Watt,' bellowed the Mayor, 'it gives me great pleasure to present you with this recognition; the Future Achievers Top Talent in Energy Saving Technology award.' And he reached out to shake Mr Watt's hand. Mr Watt was already prepared for this and was wearing a thin latex glove.

Everyone in the audience clapped almost enthusiastically but on the front row of the audience, George sniggered. He couldn't help it, he'd been struck by a funny thought and the laughter inside his head made a funny snorting noise come out through his nose. His shoulders started to bounce up and down as he tried to be as silent as possible but it was no use. George put his hand over his mouth to hold in the giggles. Allison nudged him. 'What is it?' she asked but George couldn't stop giggling.

This brought black looks and daggers, not only from Mrs Watt but also from Mr. Watt who had also heard George laughing from the stage. Mr. Watt did not like being laughed at and couldn't understand what this strange little boy found so funny. Just to be sure, Mr. Watt sneakily checked the front of his trousers, just in case his zip was down.

The reason that George was sniggering was that (and George was not the only person in the audience to notice) the trophy that Mr. Watt had been so delighted to receive was called the Future Achievers Top Talent in Energy Saving Technology award. Or to use its abbreviated title, The FATTEST Award!

George couldn't believe that no one had spotted this before it was engraved on the trophy but it had to be said, Mr. Watt certainly had one of the most enormous pot-bellies he had ever seen, and certainly this was quite an achievement, judging by the other members of the Future Achievers. Maybe the other directors in the Future Achievers did realise the name of the award, perhaps they'd even made up this award especially for Mr Watt, because they were jealous of him and they wanted to poke fun at his huge tummy.

George was sure that he could see some of the directors with small smirks on their faces and some of them seemed to have covered their mouths with their chubby big hands. Were they laughing too? At that point, George lost it completely!

The self-control he had been demonstrating up until that moment crumpled completely and he burst out laughing. Then he tried to stop by putting his hand over his mouth but that just made things worse as little bits of snot sprayed out from beneath his fingers.

'The fattest award.' he wheezed breathlessly and tried to pull himself together. The other children in the class were now laughing at George's manic behaviour and indeed, his uncontrollable laughing was very infectious. The fat directors sitting along from George were, themselves, sniggering helplessly into their hands; their chubby faces even redder than before.

Allison was too scared to laugh. She'd seen another look come across Mrs Watt's face, which was no longer flushed but now a pale, deathly mask.

Mr. Watt stood on the stage, looking furious and no doubt someone was going to pay. That someone was definitely going to be George and his repayment started immediately after the award ceremony when he saw Mrs Watt talking to her husband. Or rather, it was Mr. Watt who was doing all the talking and Mrs Watt was doing all the listening.

Or double rather, it was Mr. Watt was doing all the shouting, waving his arms around and looking like his face was going to explode like an enormous red tomato. By the time Mr. Watt had stopped shouting and had stormed off out the side door of the town hall, Mrs Watt had returned to her normal dragon-lady self and was breathing her fire towards George. She bore down on him with a venomous look in her eye.

'It's not just detention for you this time, gorgeous. You will be staying behind after class every night for the rest of this week. You will be working with Mr Jolly the janitor.'

George gulped and a little bit of wee almost leaked out inside his trousers.

IX. SCOTLAND

That afternoon, George returned home from school with a letter from Mrs Watt. His mum was standing in the kitchen, at the sink with her back to the door. George slipped the letter on the kitchen table and sprinted off towards the stairs.

Before he could reach the bottom step, he heard his mother shouting,

'George Hansen, get yourself back into this kitchen right now.'

Mums always seem to have eyes in the backs of their heads. George thought, without even turning round, her super-mum senses told her that the letter was trouble. How did she know?

George trudged dutifully back into the kitchen and watched his mum reading the letter, then, without a word, she handed it to George with a sharp flick. It read:

Dear Mrs Hansen,

Due to the unacceptable behaviour displayed by your son at the Town Hall today, it is my duty to inform you that

George will report to Mr Jolly the school janitor every day after school for one hour's detention.

The reputation of the school was undermined by George's childish and disrespectful actions and any future repetition may result in suspension or expulsion from the school. I expect to see an immediate improvement in his behaviour.

I trust this punishment shall demonstrate to the boy the error of his ways.

Yours Sincerely

Petunia Watts (Mrs)

'What did you do?' shrieked George's mum. 'You know what Mrs Watt is like, everybody in the town does, and you have to go and push her too far.'

'It wasn't my fault,' protested George. 'I just thought it was funny that they gave Mr Watt the FATTEST award, that's all.'

George's mum wasn't listening. 'I've told you before; Mrs Watt practically runs that school. Mr Meadows the headmaster is never around these days and every one of the school board are all scared of the old bat.' Mrs Hansen ranted on. 'If she wants you expelled, boy, then you are out and we can't afford to move house or send you to another town. This is the only school there is in Little Pumpington, so you had better start behaving!'

George had never seen his mum this mad before and he could just stand there and nod.

'Yes, mum.' he finally said quietly but inside his heart he couldn't help feel slightly cheated.

Just then George's dad burst through the back door, his face whiter than the starchy white shirts the fat directors were wearing today. Dad looked worried.

'It's true,' he said in disbelief. 'he's gone, he's actually gone.' And he slumped down on a kitchen chair.

'Was there a note, dear?' George's mum asked sympathetically.

'Who's gone, dad?' asked George, very puzzled and slightly worried.

'Yes, he left a note. Not a long one, no real explanation or anything. I just don't understand.' George's dad heaved a huge sigh.

'What's wrong, dad?' George asked again, starting to become more concerned.

'It's your Grandpa Jock, love,' said George's mum softly. 'he's gone off to Scotland for a bit.'

'SCOTLAND!' yelled George. 'But that's impossible. He'd have told me, he'd have told you...and dad.....and....and.'

George's mum put her arms around George's shoulders and gave him a big hug. But George didn't want a big hug, he was too angry. His Grandpa Jock wouldn't just leave; he wouldn't just go off without telling anyone, especially George.

'Here,' said George's dad, 'this is his letter.' and he handed a piece of paper to George's mum, who read it out loud.

'Gone to Scotland for a long holiday. Will write soon'

'Is that it?' shouted George. 'Is that all there is?'

'I know, son. We'll just have to wait until get a letter from him. I'm sure we won't have to wait too long.' mum tried to reassure him.

George was not convinced and soon, after a very quiet family dinner, he went off to his bed early to wait in hope for Grandpa Jock's letter and to plan how he could contact him sooner.

X. MR JOLLY, TEA-BAGS AND TEETH

Throughout Wednesday at school, George was more in a daydream than ever. Mrs Watt didn't even speak to him; she didn't even ask him any questions all day so he didn't need to speak to her at all. Allison was quiet too, as she didn't want to intrude on George's all-too-obvious sadness but she gently coaxed the story of Grandpa Jock out of him, sympathised but then couldn't think of anything else to say that would help.

When the bell rang at the end of the day, George had completely forgotten about his detention until Mrs Watt said in a voice as clear, sharp and piercing as an icicle, 'George, for your insolence yesterday, report to Mr Jolly in the boiler room immediately. Your sixty minutes begins when you arrive.'

Obviously Mrs Watt made this announcement as much for George's classmates benefit as his own, hoping that the effect and the reminder of the crime and punishment would deter other children from such behaviour.

George's heart sank. An hour in the boiler room.....with Mr Jolly! This was enough to fill any small child with fear.

Mr Jolly wasn't your normal sort of janitor. Most janitors kept their playgrounds neat and tidy, stole footballs from boys who were playing where they shouldn't and kept the school warm and working properly in a handyman kind of way. Mr Jolly wasn't just neat and tidy. Mr Jolly was immaculate. He was obsessed with cleanliness. It was even rumoured amongst the children that Mr Jolly had the psychic power to detect if a pupil was even just thinking about dropping a sweet wrapper.

He was even immaculate in his appearance. Normal janitors wore dirty overalls and maybe a heavy yellow overcoat in the winter. Mr Jolly wore dark blue denim dungarees that were clean on everyday, had sharp creases down the sides and the shiniest brass buttons imaginable. He wore pink rubber wellington boots with drawstring ties at the top and he always tucked the bottoms of his dungarees inside. Sometimes he would even wear matching pink rubber gloves.

But strangely, for a man who always looked so immaculate, Mr Jolly had a dirty little secret, something he wasn't proud of but nevertheless was powerless to control. Mr Jolly's filthy habit was that he smoked cigarettes. He didn't like to admit this and would never allow any of the teachers or school children to see him smoking but everyone knew that he would regularly sneak into his workshop to drag on his poison sticks. The smell of the tobacco would waft out of the window and you could always smell the stale stench on his breath.

But the playground was always spotless, free from any litter, mainly because most of the children were too scared to drop anything but also because Mr Jolly had the biggest sweeper-up machine of any school in the country. It was as big as a small tractor with two huge, circular rotating bristle pads at the front and six smaller rotating brushes at the side.

When George arrived outside Mr Jolly's workshop besides the boiler room, Mr Jolly was lifting boxes onto a little trolley. There were about one hundred boxes and he was moving them, five at a time on the trolley, down the ramp inside the building. When he spotted George, Mr Jolly stopped working and beckoned with two of his fingers to follow him.

They walked passed the open door of Mr Jolly's workshop. George tried to have a look Inside this Aladdin's cave, since pupils were not usually allowed in here. He could only catch a glimpse of a workbench and a board on the wall with about a hundred keys hanging on it before they briskly marched passed. Next they walked passed a storeroom where Mr Jolly was moving the boxes to. The room was half filled with cartons the same as the ones outside. George managed to catch a quick look at one of them and noticed that half the cartons were labelled 'Digestive Biscuits' and the other half were marked 'Rich Tea Biscuits'.

On both types of box was printed;

'One Case x 24 Packets. Approx 50 Biscuits per Packet'

And around the side of every box was a red sticker which read,

'Damaged Stock – Not For Sale'

What did Mr Jolly need with over one hundred thousand broken biscuits? thought George.

George's dad called digestive biscuits 'one dips' because you only have to dip them into your tea once and they go all soggy and mushy, sometimes breaking off and dropping back into the cup. But Grandpa Jock loved Rich Tea biscuits. He called them the 'Lord of All Biscuits' and it was precisely because they went all soggy that he liked them so much. 'A drink's too wet without one,' Grandpa Jock would laugh, 'especially since I've nae teeth.' and he would dunk his Rich Tea biscuit into his cup of tea and he suck on the sweet, mushy, tea-soaked biccy.

Finally Mr Jolly turned into the boiler room and said, 'I'm short staffed today. This job needs to be finished before 5pm.' and he pointed with his yellow, nicotine fingers to the ten ropes that were strung across the boiler room at shoulder height. Sadly, they were at Mr Jolly's shoulder height, way above George's head.

He then explained exactly what George had to do and George just stared at him in disbelief. At first, he couldn't believe Mr Jolly was 'short-staffed'. He didn't have any staff; he did everything in the school himself.

And George couldn't believe the job he was being asked to do.

In the centre of the room were four large boxes. They were made of cardboard and the corners of the boxes were wet, as if something dark brown was leaking from them. George couldn't lift or move the boxes as the bottoms of the boxes were wet and the cardboard would tear if he picked them up. Mr Jolly was quite specific about that.

Inside each box were hundreds and hundreds of soggy tea-bags. Mr Jolly explained that these were from the teachers' canteen and since the price of supplying electricity to the school had gone up and the budget for tea-bags had gone down, cut-backs were necessary. The teachers would have to make do with used tea-bags.

George had to take the sodden tea-bags one at a time and pin them up on the thin ropes stretched across the boiler room, with clothes pegs. The heat in the boiler room would dry them out over night and they could be used again.

'There's plenty of flavour left in them bags yet.' spat Mr Jolly as he left the room.

For the next 45 minutes George ran back and forward from the boxes to the ropes with handfuls of dripping tea-bags. He'd filled his pockets full of pegs and he found he could actually carry about six tea-bags in one hand and still peg them up with the other.

To make a game of it, George began to time himself and discovered he could hang up to fifty tea-bags a minute. Next he played at alternating the colours of the pegs, then he tried to count how many tea-bags he could hang on each rope. His record was ninety seven tea-bags on one line and George reckoned this was because he'd filled that rope up with square tea bags, which were a little bit narrower than the round ones.

The only trouble was that the ropes were quite high up and he had to stand on his tip-toes to reach properly. Soon his arms and shoulders began to ache but he pressed on, hoping to finish before 5pm so he could have a bit of a rest. And he'd have to wash his hands properly too, as the wet tea-bag juice had been leaking through the perforations in the little bags and had stained his hands a light brown colour.

At a quarter to five, George had finished his onerous task and he went over to a sink, which was in the corner of the boiler room, beside an old wooden cupboard, to wash his hands. George started to scrub but no matter how hard he washed, the brown stains on his fingers did not come off. Maybe it would be better if he used soap, he thought.

Unfortunately, there was no soap lying in or near the sink, so George started to look around for some. Maybe in the cupboard, he wondered.

The cupboard was stiff to open. It wasn't locked but it felt as if the old wooden doors had warped over time. George pulled hard, still nothing. Then, with an almighty tug, which rocked the cupboard on its base, the doors opened wide. The cupboard tipped forward a few inches and George was hit by an avalanche of dozens of pairs of false teeth!

Top sets, bottom sets, whole sets, half sets; pink plastic gummy looking parts and pearly white rows of teeth. More and more false teeth kept cascading onto George's head. He'd stumbled back with shock and fell onto his bottom as the falsies kept coming. He tried to scramble backwards but each time he moved his hands, he put them down onto another set of gnashers that were scattered around him and it felt like he was being bitten. He stood on them, he sat on them and he even felt the fake choppers nibble on his fingers.

Eventually George had pushed himself back against the far wall and he stared at the mountain of plastic dental plates that were covering the floor. The cupboard had swung forward and now rested on the doors at a slight angle. There were teeth everywhere.

George stared in amazement. Why would there be so many false teeth in a school? George only knew one boy in the school who had a false tooth, not even a full set of false teeth; just one and he'd lost that when he flew over the handlebars of his bike and used his face as a brake.

Even if all the teachers wore false teeth, they wouldn't need that many. This amount of teeth would give every teacher in the school a new set of gnashers for every day of the week and there would still be some left over.

And why is Mr Jolly the janitor keeping all these false teeth in his boiler room? What did he use them for? Maybe Mr Jolly was like the tooth fairy? Maybe he was a false teeth collector, maybe it was his hobby. But who do they belong to and who would want to chuck away their choppers?

Urrgh...maybe they were from dead people! George shuddered.

Wherever they came from and whomever they belonged to, George did not fancy being caught by the deranged janitor, up to his ankles in Mr Jolly's false teeth collection so he jumped to his feet quickly, pushed the cupboard flat onto the floor again and began stuffing the 'falsers' back onto the shelves.

This was not as easy as it seemed at first. The teeth weren't even; they were difficult to pile on top of each other but eventually, by laying the top sets of teeth flat on their gummy plates and linking the bottom sets together, it was possible to create a credible pile on all the shelves without them toppling over again.

George had forgotten about his search for soap and managed to get all the teeth back into the cupboard and he closed the doors quickly. Within a minute of the cupboard doors closing, Mr Jolly was back in the boiler room. He looked up at the rows of tea-bags, drying on the line and nodded his head in reluctant satisfaction.

'Well, it took you long enough, boy,' he muttered. 'I'll see you back here tomorrow after school.'

George groaned inwardly and left the boiler room.

XI. GIANTS

Dejectedly, George walked out of the school towards his house. He'd been so intent on finishing that stupid job with the tea-bags and then so shocked at being showered with false teeth that he'd forgotten about his Grandpa Jock, off holidaying in Scotland or wherever. It just felt so wrong.

George walked on until he approached Allison's house and he was a little surprised, and rather pleased to see her standing on her garden gate, swinging it back and forth.

'I thought you'd be passing about now,' said Allison with a smile, 'I thought you might need cheering up so Mum gave me money for us to buy sweets up at Mr Russell's shop.'

This soon put a spring in George's step and the two of them set off for the little newsagents on the corner. George told Allison all about the teeth and the tea-bags and the biscuits that Mr Jolly was moving around.

'Your school is really weird,' said Allison.

'I think the whole town is weird,' said George

'No, really. I mean I've only been here a week but I've never met the headmaster. Usually, when I go to a new school, the headmaster is always around, doing assembly or meeting with teachers or at least you can see him walking about the school. I don't even know your headmaster's name.'

'It's Mr Meadows,' replied George, 'and actually I haven't seen him for a while either. Mrs Watt is the deputy head and she runs the school when Mr Meadows is away to a head teachers' conference or something.'

'And Mrs Watt is the scariest teacher I've ever met.' said Allison, with her eyes almost popping out of her head.

'Tell me about it!' muttered George with an extra big helping of self pity.

'And your janitor is the freakiest janitor in the history of schools, I'd think.' Allison's brown eyes were now rolling around wildly as she pictured Mr Jolly in her head.

'How many schools have you actually been to then?' asked George for the first time.

'I think it's about ten now,' replied Allison without a hint of sadness, 'we have to move around a lot with Dad's job.'

'Where is your Dad, anyway?'

'He works for the Government. Sometimes we don't see him for months.'

'Don't you have any brothers or sisters?' asked George.

'No,' replied Allison, 'I'm a lonely child.'

'You mean an only child,' corrected George.

'I know exactly what I mean.' replied Allison.

'But it must be hard to make friends when you move from school to school all the time.'

'Yes, but that doesn't matter. You've went to the same school for years and you don't have any real friends.' Allison looked at George. 'I don't mean that in a bad way, just an observation.'

'I know,' replied George, 'I think it's because I used to tell people too much of the truth and people don't like being told that. I know I don't have all the answers but I just want to understand life's questions better.'

'So you don't try any more? To make friends, I mean.'

'Well, I've probably upset everybody in the whole school already so it's kinda hard to build those bridges again. You're just lucky that you've met me in my 'reflective' phase.'

'You're what?' gasped Allison, thinking George might be starting to become as weird as their school.

'My dad says when I'm being quiet, I'm being reflective. Like I'm thinking about things, mulling them over in my head.' said George.

'And what things are you thinking so deeply about?'

'That's the problem!' George began, 'My head seems to want to solve a giant jigsaw puzzle but some of the pieces are missing, a lot of the pieces are missing. It's as if I want to know all the answers in the Universe, from big questions like; what is the meaning of life? to silly little things like; on a clock, you've got an hour hand and a minute hand, right, so why is the third hand called the second hand?'

Allison laughed 'Or why can't you buy mouse flavoured cat food?'

George smiled, 'Yeah, that's it. I mean, whose cruel idea was it to put an 'S' in the word 'lisp?'

'That'th tho thneaky,' thniggered Allison.

'Or what's the speed of dark?' said George, growling and grinning at the same time.

'Mrs Watt wouldn't know that one either.' laughed Allison.

George was on a roll now, spitting out questions that went round his head all the time.

'Or why is 'abbreviated' such a long word? Or how fast would bolts of lightning travel if they didn't zigzag?' George wasn't giving up and he began to speak furiously.

'Or why do people say 'slept like a baby' when a baby wakes up screaming every two hours? Or can you dream about having a dream? Do milk floats really float? Why has my Grandpa gone to Scotland?' George stopped.

Allison just looked at him. George was staring ahead, his eyes fixed on something up ahead. Allison turned to check what had caught George's attention. Up ahead, just outside of the newsagents, was a large man struggling to get out of a very small, red car. He had big broad shoulders and a large head and hands the size of shovels. He also had a plaster across the bridge of his nose and his arm in a sling. Eventually, and with great difficulty, he squeezed out onto the pavement, closed the car door and stepped inside the shop. Allison turned to George. He was still staring.

Allison turned her gaze back to the car and now noticed the driver of the small red car. He was equally as big as his passenger and he had a plaster across his nose too. He also looked very squashed sitting behind the steering wheel. His arms were pressed into his sides and his huge hands were resting on the top of the steering wheel. The two smallest fingers on each of his hands had been bandaged and taped to the third fingers, with splints and gauze strapping. Allison noticed that the other unbandaged fingers and thumbs were an odd brown colour, as if they'd been dipped in paint. The driver stared back menacingly. Allison grabbed George by the arm and dragged him into the shop.

Inside the newsagents, the large passenger from the small car was standing at the counter pointing to the boxes of tablets on the shelf behind Mr Russell, the shopkeeper. George and Allison stood further along from the giant customer, in front of a selection of different kinds of chocolate bars, with one eye each on the big man and their other eyes looking for their favourite sweets.

'Those ones are good for the 'flu,' explained Mr Russell, 'but those ones are ideal for pain relief, which I guess you'll be needing the most. Been in an accident then?' Mr Russell was always quite forthright and asked questions, even when he shouldn't have. George liked him.

The big man just grunted that he'd take two boxes and he began to struggle to find any money deep inside the front pocket of his jeans. The sling around his arm clearly didn't help. Finally, he pulled some coins and crumpled notes of his pocket and dumped them onto the counter. The big man began fingering through the pile of cash, looking for the right change.

Allison spotted, at the exact time that George did, that the giant man's fingers were also tinted a light brown. The man inside the shop must be doing the same job as the man in the car but Allison had no idea what that work could be. The man paid for his medicine, lifted the boxes from the counter, stooped below the frame of the door and walked outside.

George and Allison turned to each other, then back to the huge selection of chocolate until they'd found their favourite kind, grabbed them, paid for them and they left the shop together, thanking Mr Russell. George thanked Allison too, as he looked in both directions for the very small red car.

'Why were you staring at their hands, George?' asked Allison.

'Didn't you see them, they were brown.' replied George, 'that's not normal.'

'Maybe they are painters?' suggested Allison.

'What? And they are only covered in brown paint?' laughed George.

'Well, maybe they are painting a really big brown fence and they got in a bit of a mess.' Allison was now thinking out loud, trying to come up with some solution.

'But how did they get injured then? I mean, those were two really big guys and both of them had plasters on their noses and bandages on their hands and arms.'

'Well, maybe they were painting a big fence in a really strong wind, like a hurricane, when the fence was blown down and it hurt them both, spilling paint all over their hands,' answered Allison. George laughed, 'I'm going to call you Allison Wonderland, cos that is the most far-fetched fairy story I have ever heard.'

Allison joined in with George's laughter. 'Well, I've been reflecting too,' she said, 'I've been thinking deeply about Mr Russell's paper shop.'

'Yes?' asked George.

'Well, it's a paper shop, isn't it? Why doesn't it blow away in a strong wind?!' grinned Allison and George laughed again.

George bit into his chocolate bar, and looked at his stained hands.

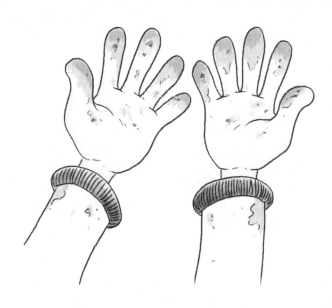

XII. POWER

The following morning was Thursday and try as he might, George could not scrub the brown mess off his hands. The tea-bags stain on his fingers had faded a little bit but not too much and he kept his hands in his pockets when he went into the kitchen for breakfast.

'Bandits!' shouted Mr Hansen, as George sat down at the kitchen table. 'Bunch of robbing, thieving blood-sucking bandits!' he ranted on.

'What's the problem, dear?' asked George's mum.

'The blooming price of electricity is going up again.' moaned George's dad, waving a bill above his head as he started to stomp around the kitchen. 'That Power Company is bleeding us dry.' he continued.

'Bleeding us dry? That's what Grandpa Jock used to say.' interrupted George.

'Well, I'm not surprised he's shot back off to Scotland. He probably saw the size of his 'leccy bill here and made a bolt for the border.' George's dad replied. 'They've got cheap power up there because of all the wind farms they have.'

'That's because of all the hot air they blow. Grandpa's well suited up there.' smirked George's mum.

'What's a wind farm, Dad?' asked George, ignoring another cheeky comment from his mother, aimed at his Grandpa Jock.

'Basically son, it's, erm, a collection of windmills, strategically placed on hillsides, to capture the wind.' announced George's dad, trying to sound as if he knew what he was talking about. 'The wind drives a propeller, which turns lots of gears and shafts until the energy from the wind is converted into electricity and captured by a generator at the bottom of the windmill.' George's dad nodded his head with confirmation, pleased at how technical his answer sounded.

'Cool! Why don't we have windmills here, Dad?' asked George. 'We've got loads of wind in Little Pumpington too. We could build a wind farm out into the sea or at the top of Plummet Point.'

George had once walked along the path that leads to the cliffs at Plummet Point with his Grandpa Jock and was nearly blown over. 'It's really blustery up there.' said George with a shudder.

'I suppose you are right, son. I don't know why no one's done it before.' agreed George's dad. 'I've heard that many houses in Scotland have their own windmill in the garden, to make their own electricity. People didn't like them at first; they said they made too much of a whirring noise and that the propellers killed birds that flew too close.'

'Is that true?' asked George.

'Only slightly,' said George's dad, 'most of those stories were made up or exaggerated by the power companies who were worried about losing money because wind power is very cheap to generate. In the end, the most important thing is wind power does not damage the environment in the same way as burning coal does. So wind power is much cleaner.'

'But Mr Watt's power plant is very clean, dad, and they don't burn anything any more. How do they generate energy then?' George was now thinking very hard.

George always had lots of questions when he was thinking hard. Sometimes answers were obvious to him but at other times he felt like he had to scratch away at the surface until solutions started to reveal themselves. Grandpa Jock agreed; he always said he liked a good scratch. Grandpa Jock also said that searching for knowledge was like gold mining and he tried to help George dig for answers. As long as you kept digging, he said, kept searching for answers, then you had a good chance of finding that golden nugget.

'Nobody in town really knows how they do it, son.' replied George's dad. 'although I'll bet the other power plant bosses would love to find out but I don't think anyone works up at the power plant any more. It's all automated. They've even stopped getting deliveries of coal. Unless the trucks arrive in the middle of the night!' laughed Mr Hansen.

'So how does the 3P's Power Company make its energy then?' said George with frustration, still no closer to finding out the truth.

'Well, me and Mr Russell think that the 3P's Power Company discovered an underground river or waterfall or something. There was some digging going on up at the power plant a few years back and soon after they moved in a whole load of new equipment. It was then that Mr Watt came up with loads of different mad ideas to get rid of his staff.' George's dad ranted

George's mum stepped in and placed a hand on George's dad's shoulder. 'Calm down, dear. Think about your blood pressure.' she said quietly, 'And you, young Mr Hansen, will be late for school again, if you don't get moving.'

George looked at his watch, then he looked at the kitchen clock just to confirm that his panic was justified, realised that it was and grabbed his jacket and bag and sprinted towards the door. Being late for Mrs Watt's class twice in one week would deserve a punishment worse than George wanted to imagine and his imagination could conjure up some pretty horrific ideas.

As he ran to school, George began to feel very nervous at the thought of another penalty and the fluttering turned to a flustering and the flustering turned to farting and George realised that his journey to school was being aided by wind power after all.

XIII. DETENTION AGAIN

Fortunately George made it to school with time to spare, never thinking before that his own wind power could be that useful. Like every schoolboy, he found the pumping and parping noises incredibly amusing and of course, he was always pleasantly surprised by the effects of the smell to everyone else around him but he'd never believed before that his trouser trumpets could make him run faster.

George thought about his Grandpa Jock, who always found fun in passing his gas. George would be sitting around at his Grandpa's house when he would subtly detect a faint whiff of rotten eggs, the air around him would become warm and George felt as if he was then being wrapped in a blanket of rancid cabbages. He'd have to hold his breath, hold it until he couldn't take it any longer and he'd be forced to gasp in a lungful of the foul colonic explosion. Grandpa Jock said that he always found his own farts to be rather fruity.

Then Grandpa Jock and George would begin to play their Blame Game. Grandpa Jock would shout 'It wasn't me, whoever smelt it, dealt it.'

To which George would reply, 'Whoever denied it, supplied it.' And this dazzling repartee of comedy genius would continue:

'He, who observed it, served it.' Grandpa Jock would come back with.

'Whoever spoke last, set off the blast.' George would retort.

'The next person who speaks is the person who reeks.' Grandpa Jock would laugh, knowing he'd played his trump card.

'He, who accuses, blew the fuses.' George would fire back quickly but then realise that he'd fallen for his Grandpa Jock's cunning twist of words.

'So it was you, boyo.' Grandpa Jock would laugh, 'You spoke next! You've admitted it. You have been proven guilty. You are the phantom raspberry blower!'

'No, Grandpa,' George would be laughing and holding his sides by now, whilst stuttering, 'i-it-it wasn't me.'

Grandpa would be merciless at this point, 'You shall be sentenced to death by a thousands farts.'

And usually George would be laughing so hard that he would lose control of his bodily functions and emit a loud, proud bottom burp. Prrrrrrrrrrrrrp! And the two of them would set off again with hoots of laughter.

George stood in the playground, thinking about his Grandpa Jock and suddenly felt very sad.

*

The day passed slowly again for George. Allison tried to cheer him up by thinking up more ridiculous questions about the world, like they'd been talking about yesterday; the ones that probably couldn't be answered.

'Have you ever wondered what the best thing was before sliced bread?' whispered Allison.

'Or if a tree fall in the woods and nobody is around to hear it, does it make a noise?' There was still no response from George.

'Or if a husband speaks to himself in the woods, is he still wrong?' Allison giggled. Her mum had told her that joke last night when they were talking about George's universal thoughts.

George smiled but Allison knew that his mind was still hopelessly trapped by his vanishing Grandpa Jock and perhaps by the thought of detention in Mr Jolly's boiler room again.

The final school bell rang and all the children happily ran off home, except Allison who waved sadly to George from the gates as he walked slowly around to the back of the school towards the boiler room. Mr Jolly was stubbing out a cigarette and clearing up the evidence. George surprised him.

'Come on boy. We've got lots to do today. You're on tea-bag duty again,' Mr Jolly said sharply, 'and you'd better be fast about it because there's another job for you as well.'

George trooped off behind Mr Jolly, through the main entrance and beyond Mr Jolly's workshop. They went through the boiler room, passed the ropes for the tea-bags and the cupboard full of false teeth beyond to another door at the back of Mr Jolly's complex building.

Mr Jolly unlocked this green door with a small brass key and slowly opened it.

This room was pitch black and the lights took a few seconds to begin to glow after Mr Jolly threw the large switch downwards. There were no windows in this room and George's eyes took a few moments to adjust to the gloom. Inside, the room was large with six metal cabinets against two of the walls, a steel door that looked as if it belonged in the vault of a bank and next to it, a pair of sliding shutters.

Mr Jolly took out a large bunch of keys with red tags and proceeded to unlock the first three cabinets on the front wall. Above each of these cabinets was printed 'Lost Property' in faded, old letters. Unlike the wooden cupboard which was home to the false teeth, there was wire mesh around the sides of these cabinets and George could see the contents from the outside. There were toys, skipping ropes, dolls, toy guns, cricket bats, tennis racquets and the largest assortments of balls George had ever seen. Footballs, rugby balls, cricket balls, tennis balls, even golf balls.

'It's the school jumble sale next week so we can sell off all the confiscated rubbish,' Mr Jolly began. 'I want you to go through these three cupboards and separate what we can sell from the junk we should dump. Then move it all through to the main entrance of the boiler room. Do you understand?'

'Yes, Mr Jolly.' George muttered, just wanting to get started so he could finish quicker.

'Start with drying out the tea-bags. I've got work to do in here first.' And Mr Jolly pushed George through to the boiler room and he returned through the green door into the cabinet room.

George started on the four big boxes of tea-bags the same as yesterday, his already stained brown fingers becoming darker. This time George discovered that if he unhooked one end of each of the ropes that were strung across the room, he could pull each rope downwards to just above the boxes, making it easier for him to clip the tea-bags onto the line without having to stretch. This doubled the speed at which he could hook the tea-bags on.

After about ten minutes of work, George heard a shout that sent shivers down his spine.

'Mr Jolleeee!' shrieked the voice, instantly recognisable as Mrs Watt from the entrance lobby of the boiler room. Mr Jolly came rushing through, muttering to himself under his breath, then to George 'Keep working!'

Two seconds later George heard the two of them talking in low, whispered tones and after a moment or two; George plucked up the courage to want to listen in. He crept quietly around the big boxes of tea-bags and put his ear close the door that wasn't quite closed properly.

'And I've given you the boy because you are running behind.' Mrs Watt was pointing her finger at Mr Jolly repeatedly.

'I still don't like it, Mrs Watt,' replied Mr Jolly, shaking his head, 'I said to Mr Watt, I said he's too close to the track, he is.'

'My husband and I are not worried about that. Potato-head through there is too stupid to work out what's going on. Just keep him busy. We must get back on schedule. Alright?'

George was much more annoyed at being called 'stupid' than being called 'Potato-head' but he was intrigued at why Mr Jolly was nervous about him being around. Maybe Mr Jolly was worried about his priceless collection of false teeth. George smiled.

'Alright, Mrs Watt but the sooner those two knuckle-heads get back to work, the better I'll feel about everything.' grumbled Mr Jolly and he turned to walk back into the boiler room. George moved even faster than if he was wind assisted, jumped over the boxes, picked up the rope and continued tea-bagging the line. Mr Jolly walked past him without even looking in his direction. If George was unhappy about doing his detention with Mr Jolly, then Mr Jolly was equally agitated at having George working in his inner sanctum and he definitely didn't like anyone telling him what to do. But clearly, Mrs Watt wore the trousers around here.

Ten minutes more of hanging tea-bags and George was further forward that he thought he'd be, even with his little eavesdropping break. He had only one box left when another ear piercing shriek shattered the peaceful hum of the boiler room.

'Mr Jolleeee! Mr Jolly!' and this time Mrs Watt walked into the main part of the boiler room where George was sitting. She stared at him with complete disgust in her eyes but before she could speak, Mr Jolly stepped through the green door.

'Come with me, Mr Jolly. We have a problem in the main hall.'

'But...what about the.....and the boy......and the....' Mr Jolly spluttered and stammered over his words, not quite certain what to say or how to say it. George felt that his presence there was clearly making Mr Jolly feel very uncomfortable.

'I only need you for a few minutes, Mr Jolly. There's a bird trapped inside the rafters of the primary block. We must get rid of it before it does some damage.' And Mrs Watt ushered Mr Jolly towards the door. 'I'm sure that the boy here will be too busy with his tea-bags to cause you any aggravation.' Mrs Watt shot daggers from her eyes, directly over to George and she and Mr Jolly left the boiler room.

George crept over to the door and watched them walk over to the primary building and go in through the main door. George's heart had been beating fast since his eavesdropping episode and this adrenalin made him feel braver than ever. He stole back across the boiler room and went into cabinet room to see what Mr Jolly had been doing.

The three cabinets with the confiscated toys and balls were still open, waiting for George to begin to clear them out and on the far wall the three other cabinets were still locked. George quickly stepped over to these cabinets, intrigued to see what treasures lay inside them. It wasn't toys. It wasn't balls, it wasn't even false teeth.

Lying flat across every one of the long cabinets, on the bottom two shelves were dozens of walking sticks of all shapes and sizes. Some were wooden, some were metal, some were plain and others had ivory handles shaped like dog's heads or amber jewels on the top. There were even a few metal hospital crutches.

But it was the items on the top two shelves that caught George's attention. Some of these items glinted slightly; some of them may have even gleamed once, when someone took care of them and a few of them had leather straps. A few were working but most looked like they hadn't worked for years.

On the top two shelves were piles and piles of watches. Hundreds of them. Gents wrist watches, ladies wrist watches, digital watches and there was even a gold pocket watch on a chain, lying to the side. George thought that the pocket watch looked exactly like the one that white rabbit carried when he ran down the hole.

'I must remember to tell my Allison Wonderland about that one.' he thought to himself as he checked the cabinet doors.

They were all locked.

George stopped. His ears were straining to hear a sound off in the distance. It was coming from the main entrance; it felt as if it was coming from under the floor. Just then George heard a soft 'sshhhhhhhhhhhttt!' sound and a draft of air blew out across his feet from under the two sliding doors.

George stepped over to them. There were no handles on these doors, no obvious way of opening them, from this side at least. They look like elevator doors but there were no buttons at the side to press and no panel to tell you which floor the elevator might be at. George looked across at the large bank-vault door to the left. It was made from cold grey steel and had a large wheel in the centre, like the helm of a ship.

George quietly grasped two of the six handles protruding out from the wheel and gently turned. From inside the door there was a clunking, knocking noise as the bolts slid out of their housing and withdrew into the door itself. The door began to swing open.

George gasped. He realised that Mr Jolly was working down here and had closed the door but not locked it when Mrs Watt had shouted him. He was expecting to come back through here straight afterwards, like the last time. He was not expecting Mrs Watt to march him off to the primary building.

George looked behind him, checking that Mr Jolly wasn't coming back right then and with a deep breath he opened the heavy door to its fullest.

XIV. THE TUNNEL

Beyond the frame of the door there were twelve metal steps going down into the blackness. As George's eyes became sharper in the dark, he began to make out a large pod, like a giant bean sitting in the corner, against the wall. Coming out from underneath this pod, on the ground was a rail made of polished metal, and this track stretched all the way down into the darkness and under the school.

The pod was jet black with clear Perspex panels at the top. There was a door in the side and when George stood on his tip-toes he could see that the pod was big enough to seat two people, like a little train. He stretched on the tips of his feet, peering into the black capsule but he soon began to pitch forward. George rocked on his toes and reached out to stabilise himself. Two things happened.

First of all, as he touched the side of the pod to steady himself, it wobbled back and forth. Secondly, the door of the capsule hissed and popped open, revealing the main seat and simple control panel inside. George jumped back quickly but in the next moment, he reached forward with his arm again to push the small panel on the door to close it. The door hissed and quietly sealed itself again.

George dropped to his hands and knees to look under the bubble-train. When he touched it, the pod didn't seem stable and George was curious why there seemed to be no weight in it at all. George's eyes widened when he saw the pod was floating about an inch above the centre rail, hovering in place. George pushed the bottom of the vessel and it bounced back and forth, readjusting its centre of gravity directly above the rail again.

'It must be magnetic!' whispered George to himself. 'But where does it go to?'

George looked behind the pod at the short wall at the bottom of the steps. There was a metal panel on the wall, about six inches wide. When George touched it, he felt the box gently humming. Moving his head to an angle, George saw a yellow and black safety sticker on the front of the panel and he squeezed his head closer. The sticker read;

'Caution - Compressed Methane – Keep Clear'

George turned back to the steps and saw a large, black storage tank under the stair well which was also marked with a sticker that said 'Danger – Methane'. Off to the left of the stairs there was a platform on the ground. At waist height, there was a large control panel with two buttons on it; one green and one red. These obviously controlled the platform and moved it from the ground up to the two sliding doors directly above. George reckoned that the elevator doors would open automatically when the platform reached the top. George was desperate to touch the green button to see exactly how this worked but he thought that the noise would bring Mr Jolly running.

Mr Jolly! He'd be back any second and George did not want to be trapped in this tunnel when the mad janitor came back. George turned towards the stairs and put his hand on the railing at the side to pull himself up.

At that moment there came a whining, screeching sound that seemed to surround George and bite him to the bone. The very air around him vibrated and George felt his chest throb. He put his hands over his ears as the shrieking became louder, echoing and bouncing off the walls and a drumming, pounding noise started inside his head.

Eeoowweey BOOM BOOM BOOM Eeeohheyyooow BOOM BOOM BOOM Eeeohoyyooww!

Terrified, George ran up the stairs and closed the large door behind him, spinning the wheel back into place. The frightening noise was almost silenced when George shut the vault door and completely quiet by the time he closed the green door and sprinted back through to his tea-bags and boxes. He quickly began pinning them back up again as calmly as possible.

Within two minutes of George's return to the tea-bag hanging Mr Jolly marched in, full of fluffy, self importance and looked around the room.

'What was that noise?' he demanded.

'What noise?' replied George, trying to look as innocent as possible.

'That screeching?' he said, 'I heard it outside but....' Mr Jolly turned his head, listening intently to the silence. 'I thought it came from inside here as well.' He turned around, now talking to himself more than to George.

'It stopped when I came in,' Mr Jolly looked very puzzled, 'or maybe it was only outside all the time.'

George shrugged his shoulders and Mr Jolly the janitor stumbled passed him into the cabinet room. Two seconds later he popped his head back into the boiler room, stared at George then disappeared, banging the door shut behind him.

George pinned the last tea-bag onto the line and hung it back onto the wall. He walked casually up to the cabinet room door, (George had no intention of washing the tea-bag stains off his hands today, one drenching with false teeth this week was quite enough). George knocked on the door and a few seconds later Mr Jolly opened it a couple of inches and poked his head around.

'Yes?' he shouted, obviously angry at being disturbed.

'Well, I've finished the tea-bags,' said George, 'and I thought you wanted me to sort through those old toys for the jumble sale.'

'No, no, it's quite alright, I'll do it. You can go now.' And Mr Jolly slammed the door shut in George's face.

XV. GRANDPA JOCK'S HOUSE

George was slightly bemused but not disappointed by the abrupt end to his detention. He was also still in a state of shock about the discovery he made behind the bank-vault style door in the cabinet room, the magnetic pod-train on the single rail track and the origin of the screeching, wailing noise that drove him out of the tunnel.

He pondered these things as he walked out of the school gates and up the road. Was he above the tunnel now? Where did it go to? Did it stop underneath the school or go onwards somewhere else?

Soon George passed Allison's house. She wasn't on the gate as she was yesterday and he felt a bit sad about that. George felt a twinge of disappointment inside of him and he tried to convince himself it was because he was hoping Allison's mum would have given her some more money to buy chocolate and not because he secretly liked her, even just a little bit.

He walked on towards his own house and saw his mum coming out of the gate, just as he turned the corner.

'Ah, there you are, George,' she said, 'you're just in time to do a little job for me. Go round to Grandpa's house and borrow his tape measure; I can't find your dad's anywhere. I think Grandpa keeps it in his toolbox, in the cupboard under the stairs.'

And without saying a word, George turned and started to walk back to his Grandpa Jock's house. As he reached the corner of his street, George's mum shouted to him. 'Your dad locked his back-door but Grandpa keeps a spare key under the...'

'Yes, mum!' said George quickly, trying to stop her revealing Grandpa's secret hidey-hole. He didn't want the whole street to hear where Grandpa Jock hid his spare key and George thought his mum was being quite careless. She'd make a dreadful spy.

George turned the corner again, sauntered down the pavement and crossed the road towards Grandpa Jock's cul-de-sac. It would be strange to go into Grandpa Jock's house without him being there and George felt the hairs on the back of his neck stand up at the thought. George still didn't believe that his Grandpa had gone off on holiday and it annoyed him that his mum and dad still seemed to think he had. He'd been away three days now and he still hadn't called to say he'd arrived safely. Mum said it was because there were parts of Scotland that didn't have telephones or mobile phone signals.

Up to his right, he saw Allison standing on her gate, looking off in the direction of the school so she had her back to him. She was waiting for him again, not realising he'd gotten out earlier. George felt a warm fuzzy feeling and tried to convince himself that he'd just appreciate the company at Grandpa Jock's house, rather than go in alone. And anyway, Grandpa Jock liked Allison so George thought that he wouldn't mind.

George shouted out, 'Hey there!' and he waved across. Allison turned, saw George and opened the gate. As she walked down to meet him, she called, 'How did you escape so early?' smiling broadly and staring into George's troubled eyes.

George told her the whole tale about the toys, the watches and the walking sticks. He told her about the strange whispered conversation between Mrs Watt and Mr Jolly and finally about the little shuttle pod, the magnetic rail track and the howling tunnel.

'That's impossible!' she cried, 'what's all that doing there?'

'I've no idea,' said George, 'but I'm not going to ask Mr Jolly about it. I've got one more day of detention tomorrow and I never want to set foot in that weird place again.'

'I'm not surprised,' agreed Allison, 'the man collects false teeth, for goodness sake!'

They soon arrived at Grandpa Jock's house and they walked around to his back door. Just to the side was a small ornamental garden with plant pots and flowers and a little garden gnome sitting on a toadstool with his fishing rod. Allison had seen the gnome the first time she'd been round to Grandpa Jock's house but hadn't paid it any attention. George went over to the gnome and twisted his little red hat until it snapped off in his hand.

Allison gasped. 'You've broken it.' she said.

'No, silly,' said George smiling as he pulled out a small brass object, 'this is where Grandpa hides his spare door key.' George moved past Allison to the back door and unlocked it.

'But I don't know why he needs a spare key. When he was in the army he says that he learned to pick any lock with just a paper-clip.' George was whispering now.

The two of them crept into the house. It was dark, quiet and very grey. George's dad had closed the blinds in the kitchen and the curtains in the living room making the whole house seem drab and sombre. The only noise was the ticking of the clock on the mantelpiece above the fireplace.

George walked carefully through the living room and into the hall beyond. Allison followed, glancing around her. Grandpa Jock's living room was a curious collection of old and new. On the wall there was a painting of a magnificent stag on the side of a mountain, which Allison guessed was in Scotland. At one side of the mantelpiece was an old wooden clock that ticked noisily and at the other side was Grandpa Jock's white I-pod, in a silver docking station.

Beyond the living room there was a cupboard in the hall, right beneath the stairs so it was quite high at one end but lower at the other. There was no light in the cupboard. 'Why do I need a light in the cupboard?'

Grandpa Jock used to say, 'I know where everything is.' so it was very dark inside.

Hanging on the back of the door were two coats, one hat and a scarf. Inside the cupboard, on the floor were old boxes of newspapers, two suitcases, a vacuum cleaner and dozens of pairs of old shoes and slippers. There was a stale, musty sort of smell and Allison wrinkled her nose up. George sneezed with the dust and recognised the odour of his Grandpa's foot powder. He thought better of telling Allison. On the wall at the back hung more coats, jackets, scarves and Grandpa Jock's bagpipes.

'I think Grandpa's toolbox must be right at the back,' said George, beginning to pull things out. 'Can you help me get this stuff?' and he passed out the vacuum and the suitcases. Allison put them behind her to keep the doorway clear. George was on his hands and knees now, crawling to the deepest darkest part of the cupboard, right under the lowest stairs. The coats and the bagpipes were swinging above him on their hooks. The chanter of the bagpipes kept clunking him on the head and the heavy coats were blocking out any light that might penetrate to the back of the recess.

'We'll have to move these out too.' said George and still kneeling, he lifted the two biggest coats and the bagpipes and passed them to Allison, who reached in and took them from George, wrapping her arms round about them. She laid them all on the floor next to the suitcases.

'Found it!' came a muffled shout from the depths of the cupboard and Allison heard the clip of the latch on a toolbox and seconds later George's hand shot out of the darkness clutching a tape measure and he handed it to Allison. Allison took it and clipped it onto her belt.

'Now give me all that stuff back in.' grunted George and Allison passed him the older of the sturdy, leather bags. As George stored the cases against the wall, he said out loud, 'I wonder why Grandpa Jock went on holiday without his favourite suitcase?'

'Maybe he was travelling light.' said Allison helpfully but George stuck his head out of the cupboard with a bemused look on his face.

'But why would Grandpa Jock go to Scotland, of all places, without his bagpipes?' puzzled George. At that moment Allison turned to pick up the bagpipes. She took hold and lifted the bag part and chanter together. The rest of the pipes started to fall around as if they were doing a crazy dance on their own. Allison made a grab for them.

Just then, Allison's foot got caught in one of the pockets of a large coat that was lying on the floor. She stumbled forwards, tripping over the vacuum cleaner, twisting awkwardly and holding out the bagpipes to break her fall. The vacuum cleaner tipped over and the handle bumped against the other suitcase. The bagpipes hit the floor with a thump, followed by Allison who landed right on top of them. Luckily, the soft tartan bag cushioned her fall but it wheezed as all the air was pushed out.

From inside the cupboard, all George heard was,

'Boom, Thud, Eeeeoooohoheeeeyyyooowwwwww,' and the pipes were squeezed into silence.

'Well, help me up then!' yelled Allison, fighting her way out from underneath two jackets; one foot trapped in a coat, the other foot waving around madly in the air, tied up in electric cable from the vacuum and the rest of the bagpipes twisted around her.

George sat motionless in the cupboard, staring into the darkness. By the time Allison had untangled herself from mass of overcoats, electrical cable and a so-called musical instrument that seemed to have a life of its own, she was not impressed. She stood in front of the cupboard door and roared, 'Some gentleman you turned out to be! I'm lying there, fighting for my life with a killer set of bagpipes and all you can do is....'

George ignored her. He was lost in thought, oblivious to anything Allison was saying. He packed away the remaining items and walked towards back door. Allison followed him, trying to catch his eye at every opportunity. They both stepped outside; George locked the back door and slipped the spare key under the gnome's little red hat again. They went out through the back gate and down to the pavement at the end of the cul-de-sac. George led the way towards the little wooded glade, scattered with a few trees and the large fallen tree trunk that was worn almost smooth.

George's head turned upwards to the sky. He stopped and looked at Allison with eyes as clear blue and piercing as daggers of ice, yet George's face had a look of serene wisdom about it, as if all the answers to life's mysteries had been explained to him at once.

Then he broke the silence. 'I know where my Grandpa is,' he said calmly. 'My Grandpa Jock is not in Scotland. He's been kidnapped and he's being held at the end of the tunnel under the school!'

XVI. REVELATIONS

'What?' shrieked Allison, 'Are you mad? Where did that hare-brained idea come from?' She went on, 'it's no wonder your mother thinks your imagination gets you into trouble at school. That's a beauty, George!'

George just stared at her. His mum would sometimes go off her head like this and George found that it was best to let her run out of steam, without interrupting.

'No, really, George. That's a classic,' Allison was getting into full flow now, releasing all her bottled up frustrations following the fight with the bagpipes, 'without a shred of evidence, you've come up with the most incredible, the most unbelievable, and the most flimsy, flaky, far-fetched bag of balderdash I have ever heard in my life.' She stopped for breath, breathed and started again.

'It's absolute insanity. The men in white coats will come and take you away, for sure. You'll be locked up if you ever mention madness like this. They'll think you have a mental disorder.'

She drew another breath.

'And to think I wanted to be your friend. You've got a nerve calling me Allison Wonderland for my fairy story. You should be called Gorgeous George the Gibbering Jackass for this fruit-loop lunacy!' She stopped.

George turned and walked away. Allison realised immediately that she'd gone too far and she chased after him.

'Wait!' she called, 'wait up, George, I'm sorry. I didn't mean it!' and she caught up with George and took hold of his elbow. He pulled away and started walking again. Allison skipped passed him.

'I'm really sorry,' she said again, 'I shouldn't have said that, George. It was really horrible of me and I wish I could take it back. I do want to be your friend.' George stopped and looked at her. He had tears in his eyes.

Allison apologised again, 'I'm sorry, George. I should have guessed you'd never say anything like that if you hadn't thought it through properly,' she went on, 'I just wouldn't want you to get into trouble with Mr Jolly or Mrs Watt. They'd go crazy if you mentioned something like that. You've had enough detention already.'

'No, we can't tell anyone!' insisted George, turning sharply.

'Well, help me understand what you're thinking,' Allison now spoke softly, as if to reassure him. 'I want to believe you but it just sounds so incredible.'

'No, it all makes perfect sense now. Well, most of it. But I need help to prove it.' George was willing Allison to say 'yes' without actually asking her directly. This had to be Allison's decision as George knew the trouble they could get into.

'I want to help you, George, you're my friend but you'll have to convince me that it's real first.' whispered Allison and she pulled George over to the fallen tree trunk and they sat down.

George took a few moments to pull his thoughts into some semblance of order. If he blurted them out madly, Allison would think he'd lost the plot. He took a deep breath.

'Last Sunday night, I saw two large men go into Mr Swan's house, opposite mine, and put a large, bulky object in the back of their van. I couldn't see what it was; they had a sack.' George paused but Allison urged him on.

'In the morning Dad told me that Mr Swan had gone off on holiday, just like Grandpa did the next day. Those two shadows might have kidnapped Mr Swan and Grandpa Jock as well!' George paused, wondering what to say next. Allison coaxed him,

'Go on, what else?'

'I found it strange today, that Grandpa Jock would go on holiday without his favourite suitcase and definitely not without his bagpipes. Not to Scotland.' George scratched his head and rubbed his hands around the back of his neck.

'Then today, when you fell over, the noise, it was...' George shook his head.

'What is it, George?'

'That noise. It was the same noise as I heard in the tunnel yesterday. Not exactly the same but close enough. I can't believe I didn't recognise it at the time but it was too loud. I heard bagpipes!'

'Bagpipes? Are you sure? How would Grandpa get into the tunnel? Where would the noise come from if his bagpipes were in the house?' asked Allison.

'I don't know,' muttered George, beginning to think his explanation sounded rather flimsy, 'it sounded the same, it felt the same, only louder, echoing, as if the tunnel had amplified the sound.'

Allison raised an eyebrow but George tried to fill in the gaps as quickly as he could.

'My Grandpa hasn't called in three days and that's not like him, and what about Mr Jolly's cabinets full of false teeth and watches and walking sticks. That's not normal, is it?'

'Well, no,' stuttered Allison, 'but is it enough to accuse anyone of kidnapping?'

'And what about the big man in the shop with the brown stained fingers? How did his hands get covered in tea-bags stains, the same as mine?' George queried.

'I thought that was paint.' replied Allison.

'No, you said it was paint. I thought it looked like tea stains. I've had a lot of experience in that subject recently.' said George.

'But what else, George?' urged Allison, 'It's still a bit far-fetched.'

'But, what about the tunnel and the little black pod-train? Where does it go to and why does it go anywhere at all?' whined George, 'what about the biscuits and the tea-bags and, and well, just everything?'

All of his suspicions felt so real but when he spoke about them out loud, they didn't sound very convincing. It was more about wishful thinking and wild guesswork, certainly nothing concrete to go on and even less to report to his mum, never mind the police. It was Allison's turn now to be thoughtful. She had a finger in her mouth and she was clicking her nail against her teeth.

Suddenly she hopped down from the trunk and turned round.

'George, you've got one chance to prove that this isn't a wild goose chase.' announced Allison sternly. 'I'll help you but you're the one who'll be taking all the risks.'

George looked up with a glint of hope in his eyes. Allison continued,

'If you get caught....' and Allison left the words hanging in the air.

'I won't!' shouted George.

'Then this is what we'll do.' And Allison laid out her plan.

XVII. THE FRIDAY TEST

Allison was waiting for George at her garden gate the next morning as he walked to school. It was a cold, fresh morning and George's breath formed fluffy clouds as he breathed heavily.

'You all set?' asked Allison, seriously.

'Yes.' gasped George.

'Have you got everything?'

'Of course,' said George, 'why do you think this bag is so heavy? It weighs a ton.' And the two of them set off for school, looking a little bit shifty and exchanging furtive glances with each other.

Eventually, to break the silence, George said, 'Friday's test day. Mrs Watt will set us an exam in the afternoon, to test us on all the subjects we've covered in class during the week.'

'Do you think she'll ask us what is the speed of light? giggled Allison.

'Let's not open that can of worms again. That's what got me into detention in the first place.' replied George, with a grunt of acknowledgement.

'Hopefully this afternoon's detention will be your last.' said Allison, almost pleading with George to behave himself.

'It's not my fault. The old witch didn't like me pointing out how wrong she was.' said George defensively.

'Well, as your Grandpa Jock would say 'keep your heid doon', stay out of trouble and we might find your answer this afternoon.' Allison reminded him.

'I'll get my own back on her,' George hissed, 'just wait and see if I don't.'

Allison squinted at George through half closed eyes and lifted her finger to her face. She wanted to warn George against trying too much nonsense but she knew it was no use, so settled for her 'I'll be watching you' glare. George smiled at the thought.

*

As they approached the school, the bell rang and all the children ran towards their queues and began to line-up. Two teachers shepherded each class towards their appropriate classrooms and George and Allison made their way into Mrs Watt's 'terrifying teaching territory', as George had once called it, although never to her face.

They sat down at their double desk and watched the rest of their classmates file in and settle down. George noticed that there were three empty desks today and began to wonder who was absent and why.

One empty desk belonged to Daniel Lyons. He said he'd been feeling unwell yesterday and Mrs Watt even mentioned that he was looking hot, so it was likely that he had a fever or a cold or something like that. Daniel liked to think he was the best footballer and best fighter in the whole school. Outside in the playground, he was loud and arrogant. Daniel definitely wouldn't like the idea that he was ill with something as simple as 'the cold' and would probably be back on Monday, telling everyone he had a severe dose of Lassa Fever or some equally vile, tropical disease.

George wouldn't miss him today. George had fallen out with Daniel the previous year when George discovered that Daniel's full name was Daniel David Lyons, or as George called him shortly afterwards Dan D. Lyons. Dandelions! All the boys in George's class laughed at that one but then regretted it as Daniel went round punching anyone who thought it was funny. Of course George was blamed by everyone for making them laugh.

Another empty desk was that of Kenny Roberts, one of the most stupid boys that George had ever met. Kenny wasn't idiotic in an uneducated way; it was just that Kenny had a massively over-powering curiosity that generally got him into trouble when his brain was over-ruled by the thought; 'what if?' and then something usually went wrong.

Yesterday George had asked Kenny what would happen if he 'pushed a crayon up each nostril? Would they meet in the middle?' Now, to Kenny this seemed like a logical question. He didn't know if his nose had two separate nostrils or one nasal passage that spilt in two near the top. And of course, Kenny had stuffed many different things up his nose in the past; pencils, raisins, marbles, peas and even a mashed up piece of banana, all in the name of science and 'what if?' but he didn't know if his nostrils met in the middle.

So he tried to find out. Then his mum was called to the school and Kenny was allowed to leave early to go to the hospital. And now he had a day off school.

The last empty desk belonged to Laura Hardy, a rather posh little girl who thought that she was better than everyone else. She certainly thought she was more gorgeous than everyone else in the whole school and she was always flicking her blonde curly hair over her shoulder. Occasionally, her mother took her out of school for a day, when Laura was attending a photo shoot for a clothing catalogue or filming for a TV commercial. Actually, Laura was one of the children used in the 3P's Power adverts, as the terrified little girl being scared by the horrible green arm and Laura was forever telling everyone she was going to be a big TV star when she grew up.

Last year, George had been getting a little bit fed up with Laura Hardy's boasting and he told that she was already a big star.

'In fact,' said George with fake admiration, 'you're already as big as two old stars, Lynn.'

'My name's not Lynn. It's Laura.' sniffed Laura with her nose in the air.

'Well, maybe Lynn is your middle name,' laughed George.

Laura only looked down her nose at him and spat, 'Weirdo!' but it didn't stop George laughing.

Today though, Laura was probably away to one of her modelling sessions and George felt a tiny bit jealous that he wasn't missing another one of Mrs Watt's boring lessons. He'd happily become a fashion model or have a cold or the 'flu or even the plague just to miss out on the tedium he was now suffering. George, however, drew the line at sticking crayons or anything else up his nose.

So he sat beside Allison for the morning's history lesson, listening to Mrs Watt drone on and on about Henry VIII and his six wives and wishing he could invent a time machine that would transport him beyond this school and big basket of boredom that it sat in.

After lunch, things were just as bad, as the history lesson was replaced with Mrs Watt's very own repetitive spelling technique. This involved Mrs Watt writing words on the board and all the children in her class writing those ten words out in their books ten times. Very dull, and very repetitive. Every week, when the class was told to do this exercise George wished he had one of those magic multi-pens that appeared in cartoons when the character was asked to 'write out lines' as a punishment. Nine other pens would be attached to it, so that writing one word actually printed out tens words all the same.

At two o'clock Mrs Watt stood up at her desk and announced, 'It is now time for this week's test,' and she shot a look across at George, 'So we shall see who has been paying attention this week.'

Mrs Watt handed a pile of papers to a boy in the front row, who took one and passed them to the girl next to him. The dwindling pile found its way to the back of the class and Allison took two, one for George and one for herself, and was about to pass the spare ones forward when George grabbed her hand.

'Wait!' whispered George in an urgent voice.

He pulled her arm back and took the extra test papers from her. 'This is it,' he whispered. 'It's payback time!'

'No, George,' Allison rolled her eyes. 'what are you going to do now?'

George took an extra page from the bundle and passed the papers forward. Mrs Watt took the spare sheets and put them on her desk without thinking.

'You fill in your test paper and then I'll copy it,' said George quietly, writing his name at the top of one of the test papers and handing it to Allison. 'and I'll fill in this one.'

He took out an orange chunky crayon from the box that he'd given to Kenny Roberts (not one of the actual crayons that Kenny stuck up his nose) and started to write with it at the top of his other test paper in his curliest, girly writing.

'No, George, that's madness. You'll be in big trouble,' said Allison and she nudged him in the ribs. 'Mrs Watt will kill you.'

'Not till next week,' sniggered George, 'and only if she works out who it was. Now you fill in your answers properly while I fill out Daniel's.'

And George read question one.

1. Which planet has visible rings around it?

And George wrote;

I don't know but I've drawn a nice cat for you.

George continued eagerly. Mrs Watt would go mental when she read this and blame Daniel Lyons all weekend; until he was able protest his innocence and absence on Monday. Question two...

2. Select the correct suffix for the following sentence 'Jim's joke was _____ than my joke.'

a) Funnyer   b) Funnyyer

c) Funnier   d) Funnierr

None of these above.   Jim's joke was rubbish.

George sniggered and jumped onto question three...

3. What happen to the six wives of Henry VIII during his reign as king?

Divorced, beheaded, died, divorced, beheaded, and died of boredom in history class.

And so George continued, writing with his crayon more and more ludicrous answers, even declaring Daniel's unknown and undying love for Mrs Watt if she'll overlook this 'alternative' test paper and give Daniel an 'A' grade for effort.

Allison kept looking over to see what George had written next. Then she would tut, shake her head and go back to correctly completing her test paper. Finally, with 15 minutes left before the end of the exam, George reached the last question.

20. James started selling chocolate bars for his scout team. He sold 5 bars on Monday, 10 bars on Tuesday, and 15 on Wednesday and so on. If he continues the pattern, how many bars will he sell on Saturday?

None, because James is so fat he will have eaten them all

And George finished off his test paper with a little drawing of a man who'd eaten too many chocolate bars.

Without pausing to admire his work, George quickly took his test paper, the one he'd written his name on at the beginning, and started copying all the answers from Allison's sheet. He wrote as quickly and as neatly as he could, writing down all of Allison's answers, realising that time was almost up and before Mrs Watt could shout, Put your pencils down now!' George was finished and had tucked Allison's page at the bottom, beneath Daniel's fake page and his own on the top.

'Now pass your completed exam papers to the front.' shrilled Mrs Watt.

George passed their three pages to the girl who sat in front him and she passed them all to the boy at the front of the class. There was one moment of pure terror for George when the boy almost dropped the test papers at Mrs Watt's feet but with a miraculous recovery he caught the pile, tapped them neatly together on the desk and handed them to Mrs Watt.

Now Mrs Watt had 28 test papers in a big bundle on her desk and George was banking on the fact that she would not look at them this afternoon. Just then, the bell rang and the school day was over. Well, it was for everybody else in the class. For George, his final stint on tea-bag duty was awaiting him with Mr Jolly.

All the children grabbed their school bags and began to file noisily out of the classroom. George was last as he struggled to swing his heavy bag over his shoulder. As he walked out the room, he managed to sneak a glance at Mrs Watt, who sat at her desk with her head in her hands, oblivious to the noise the children had been making, only

too glad that Friday had arrived once more. For a second,
George thought that Mrs Watt began to look like a real
person. Until she turned,

'GET TO DETENTION NOW, MR HANSEN!'

And George bolted out of the classroom and along the
corridor.

XVIII. THE SIGN

Allison was in the playground waiting for him.

'I've been thinking, George,' she began, 'you said that you had to hang up about eight or nine hundred tea-bags a day, right?'

George nodded, not knowing where she was going with this.

'And there are only ten or eleven teachers in this school. Even if you include Mr Jolly the janitor and all the dinner ladies, there will still be less than 20 people.'

'So?' asked George.

'Well, that means that every one of them would need to drink forty cups of tea a day to scoop their way through that number of tea-bags and some of them might not even like tea, some of them might drink coffee.'

'Again, so?' asked George, screwing up his face.

'Don't you think forty cups of tea a day is a bit much, even for teachers?'

'So who's drinking them, then?' replied George.

'Well, I don't know that. I'm just thinking out loud.' said Allison, 'Anyway, I'll go home and get my bike and you do what you need to do.' And with that, Allison ran off towards to the school gates, leaving George to sling his heavy school-bag over his shoulder and trudge towards the boiler room.

*

Mr Jolly was waiting at the boiler room door with his hands on his hips. When he saw George, he shouted, 'Hurry up, boy! I haven't got all day!' and he grabbed George by the elbow and steered him into the boiler room. The boxes of wet tea-bags were sitting in the middle of the room again and George could see that the door to Mr Jolly's workshop was ajar. All the other doors were locked shut.

'I've got to...erm, work somewhere else this evening,' said Mr Jolly, unusually stammering. George had seen this before when he was talking with Mrs Watt. 'You have two jobs tonight. Firstly, tea-bags, as usual, but quicker today. Secondly, tidy up my workshop. I've been very busy today and I need you to put all the tools away properly. Got it?'

'Got it.' replied George.

'Can't believe I'm leaving the place in such a mess.' he muttered to himself, and then to George, 'And it better be immaculate. I'll be back at 4.30pm. You'll wait here until then or else.' With that, Mr Jolly turned quickly on his heel and walked out of the main door. George crept to the corridor and watched him leave through the gates of the school. George was now alone in the boiler complex.

He slung his big bag into the corner of the room and started work. His first task was to thread the soggy tea-bags up onto the ropes and George was now a bit of an expert at this. Soon, he was almost finished and deliberately he left about one hundred tea-bags at the bottom of the last box.

He headed through to Mr Jolly's workshop. George looked around and saw the workbench and the keyboard that he'd seen the first time Mr Jolly had brought him into the building; he saw wooden pin-boards on the walls, there was an exercise bike in the corner but it was broken and there were tools everywhere. Whatever project Mr Jolly had been working on that day was clearly a big one.

Luckily, due to Mr Jolly's obsession for putting everything in its own place, the pin-boards on the walls around the room had outlines of tools drawn in blue marker pen. George could easily find the correct spots for the chisels, the saw, the hammer and all the screwdrivers. Just beneath the pin-boards were black, plastic storage boxes with lots of little drawers to store screws, nails, nuts and bolts. Mr Jolly had compulsively glued one type to the front of every drawer, clearly marking where everything should be stored. There were even outlines drawn around the spades, forks and other gardening tools than Mr Jolly kept hanging on the walls. The man was obsessed!

George ran back and forth, grabbing tools and hanging them where they belonged. He put away all the nuts, bolts and screws back in their little boxes. He stepped around the broken exercise bike and found a plastic container box in the corner. Into that he carefully piled all the cogs, wheels and gears from the bike's innards and he laid the box on the saddle of the bike. Lastly, he piled all the larger storage boxes back on top of each other in the corner and wiped the sweat from his brow. George had been rushing around solidly for 30 minutes and he was well ahead of schedule.

He turned and stared at the key cupboard on the wall. Although there were well over one hundred keys on the board, every one was attached to a small, coloured plastic tag with a neatly printed location marked on it. George thanked Mr Jolly's obsession.

Beside the key board was a clear plastic document holder, stuck on the wall. Inside the holder was a map of the boiler room complex, carefully drawn in black pen. Different sections were marked in different colours and George could see all the fire extinguisher locations were highlighted. It didn't take George long to work out the map and where he was currently now standing. He traced a path with his finger, back across the corridor and into the tea-bag room. Beyond it was the cabinet room and behind the vault door was the magnetic track, where the pod was sitting. This was not drawn on the map however, but George saw that the cabinet room and the six cabinets it contained were all coloured in red on the map.

George looked back to the key board; there were eight keys with red tags. The first one was a small brass key; six of them were identical, thin and silver whereas the last one was a long, huge key with large chunky teeth. George guessed that the six identical keys were for the cabinets, the small brass one was for the cabinet room door and the big key could only be used for something as big bank safe or vault door.

George grabbed the small brass key and the big one and ran out of the workshop and into the boiler room, closing all the doors behind him. He crossed the floor quickly; skipping over the cardboard box with only a few tea-bags left in it and reached the green door. He was racing against time and the possibility that Mr Jolly could come back at any moment.

He unlocked this door with the small brass key. It opened easily and George congratulated himself on his guesswork. He flicked the big light switch downwards, went back into the boiler room to collect his school bag, then stepped beyond the green door and closed it quickly.

In the gloom of the cabinet room, George found it almost exactly as he'd left it the day before. The only difference was that now the three lost property cabinets were lying empty. Obviously Mr Jolly had removed the toys that had been confiscated. The huge vault door stood ominously in the corner, hiding secrets that George wanted to uncover. He ran over to the door, dropped his bag and pushed the large key into slot in the centre of the door. There was a clunk and George spun the wheel around whilst the bolts slid out of their holes and he swung the heavy door backwards.

The darkness was thick, black and silent. There was no screaming, no shrieking and now that George's eyes were adjusting to the dark, there was no pod. It was gone.

The single, magnetic track ran straight into the wall, beneath the steel box now clearly displaying the sticker that read 'Caution – Compressed Methane – Keep Clear' but George was in too much of a hurry to take much notice. The pod was gone, probably at the other end of the track, no problem, thought George. It was only a problem if the pod came back suddenly. George didn't fancy the idea of getting squashed against the wall in the black tunnel.

George stepped back across the cabinet room and opened his rucksack. He pulled out a large electric, extension cable with a four headed adapter in the end; he hoped it would be long enough. George plugged in the cable to the socket in the wall by the green door and ran the cable across the room to the vault. Through the door, pulling it almost closed, but not quite behind him and down the stairs into the tunnel where he sat the adapter on the metal platform next to the track.

Next, George pulled from his bag a big black square panel with a stand at the bottom. This was his dad's Street Party Speaker System that George had sneaked out of his dad's wardrobe that very morning. George's dad took this speaker with them when the family went to the beach or on a picnic and George had felt the house shake when Dad blasted out tunes at Christmas time.

George plugged in the heavy adapter into the extension cable and the small bayonet into the back of the speaker. George sat the whole unit upright on the platform. From the side pocket of his bag he pulled out Grandpa Jock's small white I-pod nano and quickly slotted it into the docking station of the speaker. George's hands were trembling as he did this and he dropped Grandpa Jock's small white headphones on the floor. He snatched them up and stuffed them in his pocket. George would not be needing headphones today.

He checked all the plugs one more time and pressed the 'on' button and little blue lights flashed across the bottom of the black speaker. The little white I-pod looked strange sitting inside the big black speaker but George wasn't interested in style. He checked his watch, touched the centre of the I-pod and a small picture of a pipe band appeared on the screen. George pressed 'play' and the blue volume lights flickered. The music started.

'BOOM, BOOM, BOOM' thumped the big base drum.

This was followed quickly by a crisp, strident rattle of the snare drum, high and shrill in comparison. George's fingers found the volume button and pressed 'up', 'up', 'up' until he had turned the volume right up to its maximum setting. Then the base drum came back in;

'BOOM, BOOM, BOOM!'

George's eardrums almost exploded. The noise was crashing out of the speaker and bouncing off the tunnel walls, echoing around him. He pressed his hands over his ears but still he couldn't hear himself think. His stomach was jumping with every beat and reverberation. Every muscle in his body was throbbing as the dynamic pounding of the drums crashed inside the tunnel.

Then the drone of the bagpipes started up and the shrill melody of the chanter followed. In the first few seconds George had been too concerned by the noise of the drums and whether or not his ears had started bleeding that he'd forgotten about the sound of the bagpipes. If the drums tried to beat his body into submission, then the bagpipes sharply stabbed his head with each note.

George couldn't believe the power and pitch of the music in such a confined space. He'd listened to this music many times before with his Grandpa Jock but never so loud, never with so much purpose. Each passing second seemed to last an eternity and still George hung on, refusing to switch it off and allowing the avalanche of sound to crash around the tunnel.

George pulled one of his hands away from his ear and checked his watch. He flinched as the pain blasted into his head but managed to see the time. '58, 59, 60, one minute gone,' he told himself. 'Keep going, keep going, keep going.'

Still George held on. Counting down in his mind, '48, 49, 50,' again with both hands over his ears. '56, 57, 58, one more second, one more second,' he thought, fighting against the constant, searing barrage of noise, then risking one more look at his watch. Two minutes. He hit the stop button at the bottom of the speaker.

Silence. Rushing, pounding, crashing silence. But the noise was still there, throbbing in the tunnel and George could hear his blood surging through his ears. He quickly unplugged the speaker and the I-pod and shoved them back into his bag. He slung the bag over his shoulder and stepped quickly up the stairs, winding the extension cable as he moved.

Out through the vault door; winding.

Across the cabinet room floor; winding.

Unplugged the socket from the wall; final twist of the cable, he dropped the rucksack from his shoulder and stuffed the extension inside.

He ran back over to the big door, took the key out and gave the wheel a spin. George grabbed the rucksack, jumped through the green door, locked it behind him and threw his bag back into the corner of the boiler room.

He stepped across the corridor on his toes and skipped into Mr Jolly's workshop. Both keys were still in his hand. He quickly hung them up on their hooks and ran back to boiler room where his final box of soggy tea-bags was waiting for him. George picked up a handful of tea-bags and slowly began pegging them onto a rope. His ears were still ringing.

'Calm down,' he thought, 'deep breaths.' And he blew out hard through his mouth as the pounding noises inside his head echoed. The door crashed open.

Mr Jolly, panting and red –faced, jumped into the boiler room and looked around the room. He stared at George and looked around the room again. He stepped out into the corridor and George was just able to see him as he stood at the doorway to his workshop, with his hands on his hips. Mr Jolly then walked back over to the boiler room.

'What have you been doing, boy?' he hissed.

'Nothing, Mr Jolly,' replied George, struggling to hear the words as the ringing in his ears continued. 'I tidied your workshop as you asked me and I'm just finishing off the tea-bags now.' George looked Mr Jolly right in the eyes, holding his gaze for as long as possible, trying to convince the janitor that's all he'd been doing.

Mr Jolly lifted his head back, puzzled but still staring intently at George. 'Well, finish up here and get off,' he said suspiciously and he slunk off to his workshop again. George quickly hung up the last of the tea-bags, grabbed his bag and headed out the door to the playground and across to the school gates.

*

Allison was pedalling furiously down the hill towards the school. She didn't actually need to pedal since her bike was going so fast anyway that her legs were probably not making any difference to her speed. George saw the grim look of determination on her face and guessed she had some news for him. Occasionally her bike bounced over a bump in the grass and her legs shot out to regain her balance.

'This could be a nasty landing,' thought George. He'd never seen a girl going as fast as this on a bicycle.

Allison's plan had been a simple one. Make enough noise in the tunnel and the sound might just come out the other end. George had said that the tunnel led under the school but beyond the playground and the main gates, there was only the main road, a few houses and Mr Russell's shop. After that, there was only a steep sloping field, running up the hill and the power plant perched on top.

Allison had intended to wait by the main road on her bike, listening out for any muffled sound that might have been mistaken for bagpipes. Now George was watching her careen down the grass slope on the other side of the road towards the wall at the bottom. George ran across the road, as if his help could somehow slow Allison down or at least, soften her landing.

As he approached the wall on the other side of the road, it became obvious to George that Allison was thinking about her impending arrival at the bottom. She was gripping her brakes furiously without slowing down. The wall was getting closer.

Allison threw her bike to the side into a decisive skid, still grasping tightly to the brakes and she began to slide downwards; her foot and knee, along with one of the pedals began churning up grass and dirt as she was dragged to a halt, inches from solid stone wall.

'Wow, that was impressive!' gasped George, nodding his approval, 'I mean, for a girl.'

'It came from the factory!' panted Allison.

'What?'

'Your bagpipes! The noise came from the factory.' said Allison.

George had been so impressed by Allison's dare-devil, bike-riding stunt skills that he'd forgotten that she was meant to be out the front of the school on noise patrol.

'The factory?' asked George in amazement, 'The power plant factory?'

'Yes.' replied Allison

'The-power-plant-at-the-top-of-the-hill factory?' asked George again. His face was screwed up like a question mark.

'YES!' yelled Allison.

'That one?' asked George, pointing to the 3P's Power plant at the top of the field.

'Yes! Yes! How many times 'Yes'?' shouted Allison, 'The bagpipes came from the factory at the top of that hill.' Allison was now speaking slowly, uttering every word clearly and precisely, as if George wasn't only hard of hearing, but hard of thinking as well. 'Why do you think I cycled up there?'

The penny dropped. George asked, 'Was it loud?'

Allison was relieved that George had finally gotten the message. 'Well, it wasn't deafening, it wasn't really loud at all but I could hear it from down here by the road.'

'You should have heard it inside the tunnel!' said George.

'It definitely got louder as I cycled up the hill,' said Allison, 'It was as if the noise was coming out of the chimneys. It stopped before I could get to the top.'

'Well, we said I should only play it for two minutes,' said George with alarm, 'any longer and my head would have blown off.'

'That's OK. It was long enough. The noise definitely came from the factory,' pondered Allison, 'which means that the tunnel under the school is connected to the power plant.'

'Which means my Grandpa Jock is up at the power plant!' shouted George with delight.

'Possibly...probably...almost definitely,' replied Allison, 'but we need to prove it. We need to find out why the tunnel in Mr Jolly's boiler room is connected to the power plant and why your Grandpa Jock is up there.'

'Who cares?' blurted George, 'Let's just go up there and find him.'

'Hang on, George,' said Allison, patting her hand up and down to slow George's enthusiasm. 'we don't know what's happening up there. It might be dangerous.'

'That's why we need to get him out!' shouted George.

'We will,' assured Allison, 'but we'll do this properly. It's getting dark now. We'll meet back here tomorrow morning at 9am.'

'OK,' George agreed reluctantly, 'but you'd better have come up with another good plan.'

XIX. INTO THE DARK

The following morning was cold, fresh and little bit frosty. Mist hung in the air and George and Allison's breath seemed to fog around them. They sat on their bikes at the wall where Allison had performed her emergency braking manoeuvre, looking up at the smokeless chimneys of the power plant. It was a little after nine o'clock and the two friends had been watching the factory for several minutes in silence.

'Right,' said Allison, 'let's check out the boiler room at the back of the school.'

'What? That's your grand plan?' said George in amazement, 'You've had all night to think of something and that's the best you can come up with.'

'Well, what do you suggest, then?' replied Allison, a little put out.

'At least we should check out the power plant.' said George.

'OK,' said Allison, 'but remember, I was up there yesterday and there's not a lot to see.'

And with that, Allison wheeled her bike around and set off along the road that curved around the side of the hill towards the factory building. George quickly followed her. It wasn't a direct road up the hill; it was a more gradual path up the slope and that was a lot easier to cycle than straight up the steep field, but soon they were nearing the power plant on the main access road.

Actually, it was the only access road. It entered the factory through the large front gates that sat in the middle of an imposing, steel wall running around the perimeter of the building. The three chimneys towered over the main gate and the building within. There were close circuit television cameras mounted on top of the wall at regular intervals. The building and everything around it seemed to hum. Apart from that, there was no other sound.

'Do you think someone's watching us, right now?' nodded Allison, looking up at the cameras.

'Probably,' replied George pointing at the barbed wire around the top of the walls. 'It doesn't look the friendliest of places from up here.'

'But you said no one ever goes in or out any more.' said Allison.

George had put his bike down at the side of the road and had walked off over the grass.

'Well, my dad says that no one works in that power station any more,' George called over his shoulder, 'and you don't see any cars or trucks on this road any more.'

Allison joined George and stood by his side. Over to her left, Allison looked down on the school and Mr Russell's shop and could almost make out her house on the corner. As she scanned round to her right she could see the rest of the town spreading out below her through the mist. A band of grey, brown haze hung over the town, layering the fog with clear blue sky above.

'Why would anyone want to build a dirty old power station up here?' moaned Allison, 'It's a waste of a good view.'

'But the power station's not dirty now,' replied George, 'it's almost quite the opposite.'

Allison looked at the shiny, silver walls and the smoke-free chimneys. 'Yes, but it was churning out stinky, carbon smog for years. And it will take even longer to clear the skies of that muck now.'

But George was already bored with the panoramic, if murky scenery and he'd jumped back on his bike. Allison followed and they set off around the big steel wall until they came back to the front gates again. There were no other doors, gateways or roads anywhere around the building.

'Have you noticed those cameras following us all the way round?' said Allison, 'They move.'

Yes, I saw them,' replied George, 'do you think we should knock?'

'I'm not sure what you'd say if someone did answer,' said Allison, 'Er, sorry but have you kidnapped my Grandfather and do you have him hidden in a dungeon in there?'

'It wouldn't work, would it?' replied George. 'Let's check out the boiler room at the back of the school.' And he shot off, pedalling quickly down the hill.

'Hey, that was my idea!' yelled Allison and she gave chase.

*

George reached the playground first and cycled around the back of the school. Allison wasn't far behind but George dropped out of view when he turned the last corner. She sprinted after him and shot round the edge of the building just to come crashing into George, who was standing motionless astride his bicycle.

'Shhh!' he whispered in an urgent voice. 'Look, it's Mr Jolly.'

'What's he doing here on a Saturday, and whose little car is that?' replied Allison.

'Sshhhhhhhh!'

There was a small, red car in front of the main doors to the boiler room. The engine was running and the hatch at the back was open wide. Mr Jolly staggered out of the boiler room carrying a large box; he made his way over to the car and plonked it down in the boot. He closed the hatch door and jumped into the driver's seat. The engine revved way too hard and the car lurched forward out of sight. George and Allison edged their way to the corner of

176

the building and popped their heads around just in time to see Mr Jolly drive out of the school gates and off in the direction of the town.

'He's left the door open!' squealed Allison.

'What?' said George.

'He's left the boiler room door open.' said Allison pointing across.

'So he has,' schemed George, 'let's go inside for a look.'

'No!' shrieked Allison.

'Yes.' laughed George.

'No!'

'Yes.'

'No, we can't.'

'Yes, we can,' said George eagerly, 'I've been in there loads of times. This is the chance we've been waiting for.'

Allison put her hands on her hips. 'But that's when you were in detention, George. You were allowed to go in then. Now we'd be trespassing.'

'Is my Grandpa Jock trespassing?' urged George, 'I don't think so.' And he stood his bike against the wall and ran over to the main door and turned, 'Come on, whilst the coast is clear.'

Allison looked around her, her resolve beginning to weaken until eventually she leaned her bike next to George's and ran across the deserted playground to the boiler room. George hadn't waited for her and he'd gone inside Mr Jolly's workshop. As Allison stepped in through the door, George came out of the workshop with two keys, a small brass one and a long silver one.

'No, George!' gasped Allison, 'I am not going into that tunnel. We are already criminals in the eyes of the law for coming in here.'

'And I thought you had a sense of adventure.' smirked George as he walked passed her.

'Playing a prank with a big bag of poo is one thing,' huffed Allison, 'but breaking and entering will get us in real trouble.'

'Well, I'm going after my Grandpa,' said George with determination, 'you can do what you think is right.' He opened the internal boiler room, walked passed the empty cardboard boxes stained with tea and over to the green door. As before, he used the small brass key to open this inner door and he stepped through it.

Allison's curiosity was burning inside her. George had told her all about the tunnel and everything he'd done and seen inside Mr Jolly's boiler room so Allison was desperate to see these things for herself. She tip-toed through the boiler room, staring at the tea-bags pinned up drying and the wooden cupboard filled with false teeth. She walked to the green door and into the cabinet room. George was pulling open the big vault door with the helm wheel in the middle, and Allison stared at the six cabinets; three of them open and empty and the other three locked and filled with walking sticks and watches. George stood at the top of the metal stairs and Allison moved alongside him.

'This is it,' said George, 'I'm going up there to find my Grandpa Jock. You can come with me or you can wait until I come out.'

'But we haven't brought a torch,' argued Allison, 'It's too dark to see.'

'But I brought this.' And from his pocket George produced a small purple reading torch. It was the kind that clips on top of a book so George could read it in his bed at night, under the covers. He clicked it on. A faint light shone up the tunnel.

'It doesn't glow very far.' complained Allison.

'Far enough,' said George and he ran down the steps and started off up the tunnel.

Up ahead, they were engulfed by darkness. George held up his purple torch and saw the magnetic rail shine and meander off down a very narrow, low passageway. The rail gleamed softly in the torch light for about three metres ahead but after that, there was nothing but infinite blackness. Allison set off after George and the two of them began to walk up the tunnel.

The passage twisted and turned, more like a rabbit's burrow than a railway tunnel. A giant white rabbit, thought George, but dismissed the idea of mentioning this to his Allison Wonderland. They hurried along, as fast as the darkness would allow, occasionally stumbling on the uneven floor.

'George?' puzzled Allison, 'You said there was a black rail-car in the tunnel the first time you came in here?'

'Yes,' mumbled George, 'the magnetic hovering pod.'

'Well, where is it now?' asked Allison.

'I dunno,' replied George, 'probably at the other end, I suppose.'

'Okay. So...,' pondered Allison, 'A large black train could come hurtling down the passage towards us at any moment then?'

'Erm, well,' George hesitated, 'that is a possibility. But it's not that big, sort of, the same size as a small car, I guess.'

'Well, that's okay then.' groaned Allison, rolling her eyes.

The two of them began to move a little faster but it was still painfully slow. After what felt like an hour, but was probably only 20 minutes, the tunnel began to rise steeply. This next part became a bit of a climb and George and Allison stumbled and scrambled their way uphill, occasionally holding onto the railway track to pull themselves upwards. George's little purple reading light was beginning to fade but at last he could just make out the shiny outline of the polished, black pod.

'We're here.' whispered George, looking up at the inside of another steel vault door. 'This must lead us into the power plant.' And he began searching with his hands in the failing torchlight gloom for a handle.

'I've found the wheel.' said Allison and she took hold of the handles of the tiller, as if she was at the bow of a ship. Slowly she turned the handles around; cogs clicked as the sound of the intricate clockwork mechanism ticked inside the metal casing of the door, holding several tons of steel at the mercy of delicate, coiled timer springs.

George held his breath as the bolts slid back into the door and a tiny shaft of light split the darkness in the tunnel. Whatever was behind this door, whatever had made that first blast of bagpipes and wherever his Grandpa Jock might be at this moment was surely waiting to be revealed when they opened this vault door. George could feel his hands trembling and his heart thumping in his chest. The gap in the door was becoming wider and the tunnel was becoming brighter. His eyes were slowly adjusting to the light.

Suddenly George's world was plunged back into darkness again. From behind, strong hands grabbed him around the chest and an arm pressed rough sackcloth against his face. He tried to scream out but the arm gripped him tighter and his shouts were muffled inside the bag over his head. His feet were lifted off the ground and away to his left he heard Allison struggling against another unseen captor. Her voice was smothered into near silence too.

George was being bounced around, carried under the arm of a giant, still with a firm hand pressed over his mouth. His kicking and jerking were doing no good at all as the powerful arms of the running hulk crushed into him. George felt himself being tilted backwards and footsteps clunked on a metal staircase. Upwards he bounced; twenty, thirty steps before he was levelled off and carried along the flat again.

A handle was turned, the door was flung open and George's head was bounced off the door-frame. Stars sparkled inside George's head and a sharp spike of pain stabbed behind his eyes. Then he was thrown down onto a low sofa and his head hit the wall behind him.

Second later, he was bumped by another body being dumped beside him.

Then silence.

'Allison?' whispered George.

'SAY NOTHING!' A deep voice bellowed from a short distance away.

'Okay!' Allison replied, more to George than to the booming bigmouth at the other side of the room.

George and Allison sat in silence, trying to peak out from underneath the sacks on their heads as the little pinpricks of light refused to shed any detail of their surroundings. Within a few minutes, the door clicked open, and then closed again, and quiet footsteps crossed the room, each pace being absorbed by a thick, lush carpet. The steps walked away to George's right, six, seven, eight strides. There was a wooden knock and a squeak of castors, followed by a heavy 'whump' of soft leather as a large somebody sat down in a luxurious chair.

'Remove the hoods.' ordered a new voice, full of authority and command.

Footsteps again came closer and suddenly George and Allison were blinking in the bright daylight. George's ears were stinging where the bag had been ripped quickly off his head, causing the Hessian sack to rasp friction burns onto his earlobes. He screwed his eyes up and blinked, to help them adjust to the light. They'd both been in the dark for a long time, through the tunnel and in the hoods.

As their vision returned George and Allison looked around them. They were in a large plush office with thick, brown carpet and certificates and awards adorning the walls. To their left, a window was obscured with dark, varnished wooden blinds, totally blocking out any view behind it. To their right was a huge mahogany desk, with thick, fat feet on each corner. The top of the desk was covered with green leather and the whole office oozed opulence, money, power and luxury.

There was another large window behind the desk and a plump, brown leather, executive chair was silhouetted against the sky. The wooden shutters on this window were pulled fully open and the bright morning light outside was painful to look at.

Slowly the chair swivelled around, revealing a fat, red face sitting on top of a brown suit, yellow shirt and an enormous belly the size of a football. The belly's owner was wearing a ridiculously spotty blue tie which wasn't long enough to reach his belt, lying across the summit of a tummy, looking down on two straining shirt buttons, only just holding their own.

Two podgy hands gripped the arms of the leather chair and a swoop of hair combed neatly, if rather unfashionably, over a bald head.

'So, I finally have the pleasure of your company in my factory. I hope you will enjoy it. You'll not be leaving!' sneered Mr Watt, maliciously grinning at George and showing off his dirty yellow teeth.

XX. THE MYSTERY OF THE POWER PLANT

George was beginning to recover from the shock of being jumped in the tunnel by the two man-mountains and the journey up to the office. The giants were on the other side of the room with their backs to the wall. They were the same two men that he'd seen at Mr Russell's shop buying painkillers. They were both almost 2 metres tall and probably just as wide around their barrel chests. The sling was gone from around the arm of one of the thugs but the other still had bandages around his fingers. Both of them still had plasters across the bridge of their nose.

The two big men were almost identical. They were rather a gruesome sight with a dirty tinge to their skin and they had wiry, black hair sprouting from the top of their open-necked shirts. There was thick hair growing on the backs of their hands and the hair on their heads was long and dark and tangled back into pony-tails. Their faces were round and squashed, even before they'd needed to put the plasters on their noses, as it was clear this wasn't the first time they had been broken. Dark blue bags had formed under their piggy little eyes.

'You've met the Basch brothers, I see.' said Mr Watt, extending his hand over to the giants, 'Boris and Buster are from Russia, they've worked for me for a few years. They fix erm.... my little problems.'

Allison was starting to come to her senses too. 'The Basch brothers? More like the bashed brothers. What happened to you two?' she scoffed, trying to appear braver than she actually felt.

'They had a little bit of trouble with one of the generators in the power plant.' said Mr Watt, replying on behalf of the brothers.

'Where's my Grandpa Jock?' George demanded.

'Well, actually, he was the generator who gave my boys the trouble.' replied Mr Watt, sneering at George.

'What?' said George, rather confused.

'You'll never get away with this!' challenged Allison haughtily.

'I don't see why not,' said Mr Watt with contempt, 'I've been getting away with this sort of thing for years. No one knows you're here and as we speak your bikes are being taken to Plummet Point, where people will think that you have sadly and unfortunately fallen over the cliff to your deaths. Your poor little bodies washed out to sea and lost forever.'

'Our bikes?' and Allison remembered that they'd left them at the school.

'My dear foolish child,' Mr Watt reclined back in his chair and placed his podgy hands together on top off his big belly, 'after the noisy stunt you pulled in the railway tunnel yesterday, we've been watching you all morning. First on CCTV, then at the school. Mr Jolly doubled back to the school straight after you went into the boiler room. He should have reached the top of Plummet Point by now and dumped your bicycles there.'

'But what about my Grandpa?' demanded George, 'What do you mean he's the generator?'

'Ah yes, the old trouble-maker!' Mr Watt rolled the words around his mouth like a ball of spit. 'That bag of muck on my doorstep was the final straw.'

George looked up in surprise.

'Yes, I saw the old fool from my window, jumping over the wall,' snarled Mr Watt, 'so he had to be punished. Now he is repaying his debt to society. Well, to me, at least.'

'Where is he?' George shouted.

Mr Watt drummed his fingers on his bulbous belly, 'Oh, he's not going anywhere, not after the last escapade.'

Allison asked 'What do you mean by that?'

'Well, he was rather troublesome when we brought him in, hence the first aid requirements for the twins here.' Mr Watt waved over to Buster and Boris who stared down at their feet rather sheepishly. 'Then, a couple of days later he proceeds to entertain us with his wretched music.'

'That must have been what I heard on Thursday.' gasped George.

'Yes, we assumed he was trying to raise the alarm. That is why we increased his, er... his suspension.' Mr Watt snorted a vile kind of laugh through his nose. Then he went on, 'so once we heard your rather loud reply yesterday, we knew we had to keep an eye on you both.'

'But what goes on here?' asked Allison, 'Do you really make electricity?'

'Do I? I'll say I do,' boasted Mr Watt, 'I have the greatest power station in the world. It's the cleanest, greenest, meanest power station on the surface of this planet. It is almost completely self-sufficient, produces more power than I know what to do with and generates me enormous sums of money.'

Mr Watt reclined further back in his chair and tilted his head upwards. George was expecting that any second now Mr Watt would let out a loud, maniacal 'Mwahahahahahahaaaa!' laugh. He didn't but droned on, 'For the not inconsiderable, yet necessary cost of thousands of tea-bags and biscuits every year, this station produces enough energy to power Little Pumpington and all the surrounding areas, and the spare capacity of power, I sell that energy to the other power plants at exorbitant prices. It's no wonder those jealous owners want to get their hands on my plans.'

'You generate electricity from tea-bags?' asked George.

'Well, almost,' quipped Mr Watt, self-assured and egotistical, 'and you should know, George, you've been recycling them for me.'

'It was your idea to give George detention and make him hang those tea-bags up?' gulped Allison.

'Oh yes,' he sleazed, 'The unhappy coincidence of the injuries to my boys and George's unfortunate laughter at my presentation presented me with the opportunity to combine the recycling of my tea-bags with punishment for this impudent scoundrel.'

George looked down at his tea-bag stained fingers and across to the dirty hands of the hulks, standing at the door.

'With my boys unable to work as hard as normal, it put extra pressure on Mr Jolly,' explained Mr Watt calmly, 'so you, George, were used to pick up the slack. My wife enjoyed that particular solution.'

George spluttered, 'Mrs Watt knows about this?' It hadn't occurred to George at first but seemed obvious now; they were husband and wife, of course.

'Of course she knew,' guffawed Mr Watt, 'it was practically her idea. She's as much part of this power plant as I am.' Mr Watt struggled to his feet, resting heavily on the desk and walking around it. 'Petunia, or Mrs Watt to you children, loved coming here as a small child. She loved the power and control she felt, looking down on the minions below.'

He was walking across to the dark window now, 'Almost as much as I enjoy looking down on my little generators.'

He pulled the cord at the side of the window and the wooden blinds flew upwards, revealing the factory floor below. George and Allison stood up eagerly, gripped by their curiosity to see what lay beneath.

Immediately out of the window was the high walkway. To the right was the long metal staircase down to the open-plan factory floor. This area of the power station had once been filled with steam turbines and hydro-crackers and blast-furnaces. There was a time when you couldn't move on the ground level for magnetic field conductors and internal combustion engines driving the pistons to turn the crankshafts, converting pressure into power and generating energy.

Today all of that machinery was gone. It had been stripped out and shipped off, leaving a massive vacuous, open-plan metal cavern in the shell of the former building.

Now, in the middle of the factory floor were row upon row of exercise bikes. There were at least fifty columns of bikes, securely fastened to the floor and each rank stretched another sixty or seventy bikes deep. The whole centre of the power station was filled with a square block of over three thousand exercise bikes.

George and Allison pushed closer to the glass. On every bicycle they could see an old man or elderly lady wearing a blue or a pink track suit and they were all pedalling steadily. They were almost racing; continually and consistently turning the pedals of their bikes in rhythmic revolutions. White hair nodded and bald heads bobbed up and down as the elderly cyclists powered forever onwards, staring hypnotically ahead.

Each one of the pensioners was wearing headphones and was wired up to a brown tube which was inserted into their forearms, the same as a saline drip is used in a hospital. The tubes ran down the front of the bikes, around the base and off to the side of the facility where hundreds of these pipes ran inside a yellow rotating pump with a large glass fish-tank on top. However, instead of fish swimming about inside this large aquarium, it was half-filled with sloppy brown goo. There were two empty tanks at either side of the sludgy aquarium.

Underneath each saddle was another tube, yellow this time and thicker than the first, running down the back of the bikes. These larger tubes led back off towards the school tunnel where George and Allison had first been dragged in. Of course, they'd had hoods over their heads then so they hadn't seen the huge, steel cylinder that was built into the wall at the top of the tunnel.

This tank was shiny and black, easily 5 metres tall and 20 metres long, with a crawl space on top between the cylinder and the ceiling. The words 'Septic Chamber' were written on the side. There was also a little black and yellow symbol in a triangle at the top of the tank and George thought the picture looked a bit like a squashed spider. He wouldn't have given it a second glance until he read the words 'Bio-Hazard – Flammable Liquid' printed underneath.

On the wall facing the cyclists was a gigantic cinema screen, ten metres in height and thirty metres wide. Pictures flickered across the screen and George strained his eyes to see the images clearly.

'Presenting my patented Pensioner Pedal Power Producer.' announced Mr Watt proudly and he waved his hand across the window in triumph.

'I very rarely have the opportunity to show off the inner workings of my most marvellous invention so please oblige me with your fullest attention.' said Mr Watt as he walked back around his desk, opened the drawer and pulled out a surgical mask and a pair of white rubber gloves. He slipped the elastic over his head and secured the mask firmly over his mouth and nose. A sprinkle of talcum powder fell from each glove as Mr Watt stretched them out, pulled them on over his hands and snapped them on his wrists. He squeezed his fingers together until the rubber was skin-tight snug.

With a flourish, Mr Watt opened his office door and led the way along the metal walkway. George and Allison exchanged glances and followed Mr Watt in astonishment. The Basch brothers brought up the rear with a swagger.

As soon as they had left the office, George could clearly see the enormous screen on the wall. 'That's Coronation Street!' he exclaimed.

'Yes,' said Mr Watt, muffled behind his mask, 'we like to keep our patrons entertained with continual repeats of all the soap operas, as well as classics such as 'Murder She Wrote' and 'The Antiques Roadshow'. We find that it helps boost productivity.'

'Productivity?' balked Allison, 'what do your patrons produce?'

'Why, electricity, of course!' beamed Mr Watt, his eyes glazing over as he filled up with tears. 'This is my proudest achievement. Simple, self-sufficient, perpetual energy.'

'And how many...er...patrons do you have here?'

'I think we are over the three thousand mark now. My boys have been busy almost every night for the past five years.'

'And no one has noticed?'

'I believe my advertising campaigns have brainwashed enough people to carefully avoid any difficult questions being asked. Did you like them? I designed those posters myself, you know.'

'I think he's mad,' whispered George to Allison.

'Just humour him.' said Allison quietly until two large hands pulled them apart from behind.

'This is, er, incredible,' said George in false admiration and growing courage, 'how does it all work?'

'How does all work? You want to know how my power station works?' Mr Watt's voice was beginning to tremble at the prospect of sharing his vision. Any hatred that Mr Watt had shown towards George had disappeared and he seemed to bask in the glow of his achievements.

'Clearly, we have entertainment for our patrons, as you can see we have our deluxe, state of the art cinema screen. This is viewed from the gallery where the patrons are safely strapped onto their Powerambulator 2000. Generally, this must be pedalled at an average rate of no less than 120 revolutions per minutes,' explained the wide-eyed Watt.

'What happens if the, er, patron wants to slow down or just stop pedalling?' asked Allison, opening her eyes inquisitively, hoping to fool Mr Watt.

'Well, the patrons are then encouraged to continue pedalling with a 12 volt charge of electricity directly into their nervous system. This normally kick-starts their positive contribution to our grid.'

They began to walk to down the staircase, Mr Watt still marvelling at his insane accomplishments. 'It's actually very simple. The pedalling motion on all the bikes is wired through a large junction box with a power inverter using ultra-capacitors to smooth out the energy flow into the generators and the......'

George thought to himself, 'He's absolutely mental. He's completely and utterly barking mad!'

'And this routes through to the feeding station,' Mr Watt went on, 'which supplies our patrons with all their nutritional requirements, together with the additional muscle growth stimulants.'

'Is that the brown sludgy stuff over there?' asked Allison, trying to sound as interested as possible. Mr Watt looked at her out the corner of his eye and shuddered.

'That brown sludge, as you call it, stupid girl, is a specially blended recipe of infused Camellia Sinensus, together with essential wheat flour, sugar and malt.' said Mr Watt impertinently.

'So,' replied Allison, equally precociously, 'It's tea and biscuits then.'

'That's why I was drying out all the tea-bags,' gasped George, 'the recycling saves you money.'

'Of course,' replied Mr Watt, 'all such efficiencies are necessary in a commercially astute business operation.'

'But why do you need muscle growth?' asked Allison.

'See for yourself,' replied Mr Watt, reaching the bottom of the stairs and striding towards the rows of exercise bikes and his patrons.

As George and Allison walked closer, they saw that the old people cycling were in a trance-like condition, staring ahead but not truly seeing. They all moved in simultaneous motion, at the same speed and almost in unison. That's when George noticed;

'Look at the size of their legs!' he yelled.

Beneath the blue or pink tracksuit bottoms, Allison now saw that every cyclist had calf and thigh muscles equivalent to an Olympic athlete, bigger even. Their legs were like body builders'; every muscles and sinew developed to its maximum. Some of the men had thighs thicker than George's waist, some of the women's legs were so thick that the tracksuit material was stretching and straining over the bulky flesh, ready to burst.

'The stimulant that I use was originally designed for beef cattle, to promote muscle growth,' Mr Watt went on proudly, 'but as you can see, it works equally well here, promoting power, strength, and stamina. We also add a relaxant, to...er... make our people more...er...compliant, more willing to help.'

'They're drugged.' whispered Allison.

Mr Watt marched around behind the last row of cyclists, followed by the gawping George and Allison with Boris and Buster bringing up the rear.

'These are my oldest patrons; they've been here for over 5 years,' said Mr Watt. 'When I first struck upon my grand plan of removing the least power-consuming element of our society and re-engaging them in power-generation, I was fortunate to acquire a bus-load of potential pedallers out on a day trip. I simply arranged for their families to believe that they had all gone off to Africa to become missionaries. No one asked any questions, no police enquiries and no fuss. Over the course of a year, I redeveloped my power plant to transfer from fossil fuel to pedal power and Boris and Buster have been securing the services of more perambulators ever since.'

Mr Watt talked as they walked along the end row of the elderly bikers. 'As you can see, these slightly newer additions have less muscle growth than the earlier examples.' George and Allison saw that, as they walked further along the rows, the smaller the thighs of the cyclists became. Mr Watt went on, 'but in time, their physiques will advance, enriched by good exercise, nutrition and chemical enhancement, together with the fulfilment of being able to put something back into the community.'

'You think these people look fulfilled?' said Allison in amazement.

'Oh yes!' gushed Mr Watt, 'Before, they were seen as a burden on their families and on society. Now they are making a valuable contribution.'

'They look like zombies,' replied Allison.

'Nonsense,' said Mr Watt, 'I'm sure that underneath their vacant expressions and soul-less eyes , deep down, deep, deep down they know that their unselfish legacy will be a world for their grandchildren, free from the pollution of fossil fuels and unfettered by carbon emissions.'

George listened to the madman go on. 'He actually thinks he's doing some good,' whispered George. 'he's justifying his actions and clearing his conscience.'

'If he's got one.' replied Allison under her breath.

'How long does everyone have to cycle for? Four hours, eight hours maybe?' said George hoping that the question would sound reasonable.

'Ha ha, very funny, boy,' laughed Mr Watt. 'no one ever stops, George. Every one of my geriatrics cycles permanently, even when they are sleeping. It becomes automatic after a while.'

They continued walking to the end of the rows.

'And as we move along, you can see some of our newest recruits.' Mr Watt happily pointed out to the last set of exercise bikes. 'Obviously we cannot expect these fledglings to begin their electrical generation at the same level as our experienced operatives so they only need to pedal at 40 revolutions per minute but this quickly builds up.

'There's Mr Swan!' shouted George, pointing over to the old man on the end. He was wearing a blue tracksuit but he still had his fingerless gloves on. 'And Mr Meadows, our headmaster.'

'Yes,' groaned Mr Watt with a false, apologetic grimace, 'we had some...er...difficulties down at the school and we felt it was best if Mr Meadows joined us here. Petunia is quite capable of running the school herself, you know.'

'And what happens when your...er...patrons need to go to the...er...toilet?' asked George queasily.

'Very ingenious method of collection there, all my own work,' replied Mr Watt proudly. 'it's my almost-patented Super Pooper Scooper Loop!' He pointed to the thick, yellow tube coiling down from the saddles and beneath each of the exercise bikes. The tube twisted into a dirty metal slop pan at the bottom, then back out again and ran along the floor into the big, black tank next to the tunnel.

'We started by having to empty the metal bed pans by hand. Well, clearly I didn't, the boys did, but now we've fine-tuned the process to pump the pans into the septic tank. Needs a bit of daily flushing but works well overall.'

boasted Mr Watt. 'Completely self sufficient, you know. One pump in, another pump out. I even power that little train in the tunnel using compressed methane gas from the effluent.' Mr Watt went on, 'Then, once every three months, I sell that slurry to the local farmers, who'll pay a small fortune for such high quality manure for their crops. It's just genius.'

'So where's my Grandpa then?' demanded George bravely, becoming frustrated with Mr Watt's arrogance.

'Ah, the generator we had most difficulties with. Of course.' Mr Watt spread his arms wide then pointed with his rubber-gloved hand above his head. 'As I said, we had to increase his level of suspension to keep him out of trouble and his work rate is now approaching satisfactory levels. If he is able to behave himself for a further three months, he will be returned to terra firma.'

George and Allison followed Mr Watt's white pointed finger towards a yellow control box and a cable running upwards to the ceiling and saw, suspended high above the rest of the elderly cyclists, Grandpa Jock pedalling for all his worth. He was wearing an orange tracksuit and was staring blankly ahead. His sludgy tube, half-filled with the tea and biscuits mixture ran up one of the chains securing the bike to the roof, along the ceiling and down the back wall into the slopping tank.

'We put all of our trouble-makers up there in orange suits, to set them apart. Very quickly they seem to want to join the community here on the ground.' assured Mr Watt. 'And these two Powerambulators are for you.' Mr Watt smiled meanly and waved his hand towards to two empty exercise bikes at the back of the pack.

George and Allison were shaken awake from their surreal tour as the grim reality of their surroundings sank in. They'd walked across here from the office, in shock and sickened amazement, listening to Mr Watt talk nonchalantly about his demented grand plan, without realising that he was leading them to their place in the pedal power generator.

To their great surprise, Mr Jolly was kneeling behind the second bike, still wearing his pink wellies, with his spanners, nuts and bolts scattered around him. 'Almost finished now, Mr Watt.' he said.

'Bikes delivered safely, Jolly?' asked Mr Watt.

'Yes sir,' replied Mr Jolly, 'to the top of the cliffs where you told me, sir.'

'Jolly good, Jolly. Jolly good.' And Mr Watt snapped his fingers.

The Basch brothers, who'd been quietly standing behind the group grabbed George and Allison by the shoulders and held them firmly. George and Allison started to struggle but quickly realised the futility of it.

'No!' shouted Allison, 'You can't do this to us.'

'Oh, but I can, and I will,' laughed Mr Watt, rolling his eyes, 'I always knew I'd get my own back on you for laughing at me on stage.' George cringed at the thought of the Fattest Award but it was funny and even if he'd known his fate then, he still couldn't have helped himself from laughing.

'It's a shame,' Mr Watt said to Mr Jolly, 'but I can't call this energy 'Pensioner Pedal Power' any longer, not with two small children part of the plan. Eh, what?' And he took two giant sticky plasters out of his pocket and placed each one in turn, onto George and Allison's necks.

'A mild sedative,' he said casually, 'Just until my tea and biscuits relaxant begins to work properly.'

George and Allison felt their muscles relaxing and a soft calmness washed over each of them. Buster and Boris picked them both up and plonked them down, less than gently, onto the two empty exercise bikes. George had to grasp onto the handles to stop himself from falling off and Allison did the same. Leather shackles were quickly locked around their ankles and these were attached to the pedals of the bike.

Mr Jolly the Janitor stepped back, proudly surveying his handiwork and Mr Watt flicked a switch. Three little lights flickered on at the front of the handlebars.

'The green light means you're doing fine. If it's amber, well, you'll have to pick up the pace because if it turns red then.....Bzzzzz, you'll want to go faster anyway.' explained Mr Watt. 'Petunia, I mean, Mrs Watt will be along later to attach you to your nutrition drip. Sorry we don't have tracksuits small enough to fit you yet.'

The amber light flashed on the handle bars. George and Allison looked at each other and started to pedal, not daring to see the red light come on.

'Leave them to it, boys. Get the tea on.' ordered Mr Watt to the Russian brothers. Then he turned to Mr Jolly and pointed towards the tunnel, 'Back down to the school, Jolly, there's a good sport. Tidy up any loose ends.' And the janitor headed for the open vault door.

'I suppose I could call it my 'Geriatric and Juvenile Generator', now that we have children working for us.' mumbled Mr Watt behind his surgical mask as he headed away towards the stairs.

George and Allison kept pedalling faster until the amber light changed to green. They both kept up a steady pace for fear of an electric shock. A pedalling Grandpa Jock hung over them.

XXI. SHOCKS AND KNOCKS

When Mr Watt said 'get the tea on', he didn't actually expect Boris and Buster to switch on the kettle and enjoy a nice cuppa. What Watt meant by this instruction was for the Basch brothers to begin preparing the nutritional supplement for his guests.

This involved numerous trips through the tunnel on the hover-pod, bringing back boxes of the dried out tea-bags and ten cases of Rich Tea and digestive biscuits. Every time Boris made a trip in the little train, he unloaded all the boxes at the mouth of the tunnel and shot back down again towards the school. Buster then carried them over to the yellow pumping machine and the empty glass tanks.

Finally, when Boris had brought all that was required through the tunnel, from the storerooms next to the school (well, an illegal slave labour power plant could not be expected to receive deliveries of tea and biscuits through the front door now, could it?) he joined his brother in shifting all the boxes over to the central pumping unit. All the tea-bags were moved to the now empty tank on the right, whilst the broken biscuits were dragged over to the also-now-empty tank on the left.

The brothers began filling these tanks with the contents of the boxes. Boris threw all the dried tea-bags in until he'd covered the bottom of the enormous tank with a thick layer of tea-bags. Next, he pulled across a gigantic hose pipe and began to fill the tank with water. It looked like hot water too, as there was steam rising out from the top.

Buster, on the other side, was filling that tank with the mixture of broken biscuits, mixing Rich Tea and Digestives. His job took longer since he had to open each packet one by one, and his fat fingers were no good at unpeeling the 'easy-open' strip. Sometimes the giant Russian would get very impatient and begin ripping open packets with his teeth before tipping the biscuits into the top of the tank.

When they'd both finished, Buster went to the central yellow console, unlocked a small hatch-door and pulled out a large brown medicine bottle. He unscrewed the lid and poured the contents into the biscuit tank, turned back to the console and pressed the large green button on the front. The two brothers then headed off towards a door beneath the staircase towards Mr Watt's office, each munching on a Digestive biscuit.

The wheel in the middle of the centre tank began to churn slowly, throwing up the remaining yellow sludge as broken biscuits were drawn in one side and the dark tea-infused liquid flowed into the other. At first the yellow sludge turned into a sickly mixture of sloppy brown and biscuity crumble until the stirring action eventually smoothed out the whole concoction into a creamy paste. Then the pump started and the thick liquid was pushed through the tubes to nourish thousands of hungry cyclists.

From his position at the edge of the pack of cyclists George had been able to turn around on his bike almost 90 degrees to watch this well rehearsed ritual taking place. The problem was that this made for a rather difficult cycling position and on three occasions George had to quietly endure the pain of 12 volts of electricity zapping through his body. Each time this happened, Allison would urge George on with words of encouragement before whispering,

'Where are they now?'

'They're gone.'

George had been providing a running commentary of the Basch boys' activities to Allison, who couldn't see through the throng of cyclists but now the brothers had disappeared, the two friends took time to look round about them.

They were surrounded on fully two and almost three sides by pedalling pensioners. Mr Swan was there, two bikes to the right, pushing his pedals around steadily. All the cyclists there were obviously new to the power plant as they were cycling very slowly compared to the experienced veterans at the other end and none of the people around George and Allison had very big muscles on their legs.

'What are we going to do?' whispered Allison.

'I'll think of a plan later, no rush.' replied George calmly.

'No rush! Once Mrs Watt gets here and pumps us full of those toxins then we really are in trouble,' realised Allison, 'we'll never get out after that.' She was still feeling light-headed and she remembered she still had the patch of chemical relaxant on her neck. Looking around one more time, she ripped off the plaster and plucked out a few hairs at the same time. The pain quickly brought her back to their reality.

'George, take your patch off. You're too relaxed. It's stopping you thinking clearly.' But George was drifting off into a world of his own. Allison reached across to the side, managed to slip her finger nail under the corner of the blue plaster and yanked hard.

The tearing plaster pulled off dozens of the little dark hairs on the back of George's neck too and he let out a little yelp. 'Ow, what did you do that for?'

'Well, thank goodness you're back in the land of the living,' said Allison, 'and watch the lights on your handlebars. They've dropped down to amber.'

George looked down and realised that the removal of the plaster and the subsequent pain had slowed his pedal pace down significantly. The little orange light was glowing and George didn't want to risk another electric shock.

Suddenly, boing!

'Hallo, lad!'

George couldn't see his handlebars any more. Right in front of him, inches from his face had appeared two glaring nostrils and a mop of floppy ginger hair.

'Fancy meeting you here, then.' beamed Grandpa Jock, upside down.

With that fright, George stopped pedalling.

Bzzzzzzzzzzzzzzzzzzzzzzzz!! Every muscle in George's body contracted. Searing burns shot along every nerve and fibre and for a short second he was paralysed by the electric current pulsing through his body. As quickly as it started, it was over.

'Keep pedalling, lad,' said Grandpa Jock, 'I'll soon fix that shocker for you.' In his hand Grandpa Jock had his little blue bagpipe repair kit. He dropped behind the front of the bike and started fiddling with the electric motor with the screwdriver extended.

George looked up and saw that his upturned Grandpa Jock was hanging from a rope made from a bundle of plastic piping which were secured to his suspended exercise bike. George looked across at Allison, who was staring open mouthed at the ancient orange action man, swinging on sludgy, feeding tubes. Everyone else around them was oblivious to the upside down operation.

'Okay, lad, you can stop pedalling now.' said Grandpa Jock as he swung across to Allison's bike.

'Soon have you sorted, lassie.' George stopped pedalling and braced himself for the shock but nothing happened. Seconds later Allison stopped pedalling too. Grandpa Jock then switched to the scissors part of the 'repair kit' and set about picking the lock on the shackles around her ankles.

'I told you my Grandpa could pick any lock.' said George proudly.

'Where did you learn to do that?' asked Allison.

'I wasn't just a pipe band sergeant major in the army.' winked Grandpa Jock as Allison shook her legs clear, and he swung himself onto the floor and untied the tubes from around his waist. He ran back round to George's bike and quickly opened the locks on his shackles. After a good look around, Grandpa Jock whispered, 'This way!' and he darted off, threading his way through the exercise bikes towards the front of the factory floor to a little door beneath the so-called state of the art cinema screen, which turned out to be the wall of the factory painted white.

Grandpa Jock opened the door and stepped through. He held it open for George and Allison who quickly followed and he closed it behind them. It was a tiny storeroom filled with blue and pink tracksuits.

'We'll be safe here for a bit but we'll have to get moving soon, before Mrs Watt comes to tube you up.' whispered Grandpa Jock, opening a packet of Digestive biscuits.

'What are you doing, Grandpa!' yelled George.

'Well, I'm starvin' lad. I've been up on that blooming bike all night!' and he munched into two biscuits together.

'How did you know about this place?' asked Allison.

'You didn't expect me to stay up on that bike forever, did you? I stashed a box of biscuits in here a couple of days ago.'

'But how did you get down?'

'Well, what day is this today? Saturday? Right. It was on Thursday those two big eejits forced me up on that bike, the high one, to keep me oot o' trouble.'

'The Basch brothers. They are from Russia.' said George.

'Russia, you say? Well, I certainly kicked one of them in the Baltics, head-butted both of them and broke a few fingers before they strapped me into the flying bike. Knocking them about is what caused all the trouble.'

'What trouble?' asked George.

'Surely you heard my signal, lad.' said Grandpa Jock, munching into another two digestives and spraying crumbs as he spoke.

'Oh, please start at the beginning, Mr Jock.' begged Allison.

'Alright,' said Grandpa Jock, thinking back. 'It must have been Monday night, after our burning bag of poop; those two goons broke into my house and carried me away in a big sack.' He stopped talking and munched into more biscuits.

'They brought me up here and tried to wire me to one of those exercise bike things. Well, I'm no' having that, laddie.' And he winked across at George.

'So, there was a bit of a scuffle and Basch boys got a bit bashed.' Grandpa Jock sat back and smiled. 'But they still managed to lock me in this cupboard for a couple of days to cool off, kept sticking these blooming plasters on me.'

'We went to the town hall on Tuesday,' said Allison, 'that's when Mrs Watt gave you detention with Mr Jolly, George.'

'Mr Jolly?' asked Grandpa Jock. 'Is that the funny little man with the pink welly boots?'

'That's him, Grandpa,' chirped George, 'do you know him?'

'He was in here all day Tuesday and Wednesday, complaining that I'd given him too much extra work to do. He had to shovel the biscuits and fill up the tea-bag tank,' sniggered Grandpa Jock, 'apparently, those two big

Muppets couldn't come into work because of their...er...industrial injuries.'

'So Mr Jolly had to do all their work as well? No wonder he wasn't pleased.' giggled George.

'Aye, he even had to clean out the slop buckets in the afternoon.'

'Slop buckets?'

Well, there are three thousand people in there. That's a lot of pensioners pee and poop.' And Grandpa Jock screwed his face up. 'It gets rather smelly in the factory between 3 o'clock and 6 o'clock, when they pump the stuff into that big black tank.

'That's why Mr Watt is at home in the afternoons,' shouted George, penny dropping.

'My thinking exactly, lad. He's always going around wearing that stupid mask and those rubber gloves. He's obsessed with cleanliness but it's his conscience that's dirty.'

'But why is he kidnapping people and chaining them to exercise bikes, Grandpa?'

'Because he's a psychopath, lad.'

'A cycle path, Grandpa?' asked George, 'but the bikes don't go anywhere.'

'No, not a cycle path, a psychopath!' laughed Grandpa Jock, 'he's a nutter, a loony, a control freak! Always has been.' Grandpa Jock had stopped laughing.

'He's a manipulative, guiltless liar who is full of his own self-importance who has never accepted responsibilities for his own actions!' Grandpa Jock was becoming irate, working himself up.

'He thinks he's perfect! He actually believes he's better than everybody else in this whole town, the whole country, and he refuses to be beaten, even if he has to cheat to win!' Grandpa Jock's anger was now boiling over.

Allison could only stare at the ginger-haired geriatric frenzy taking place.

George said, 'Grandpa, calm down. What's the matter?'

'Calm down?! This power plant should have been mine. I should be the managing director now! Me! Not that superficial, antisocial criminal psychopath out there.' Grandpa Jock finally broke down.

'What do you mean, Mr Jock?' Allison said tenderly, patting the old man's hand.

'I went to Power Plant Academy too,' admitted Grandpa Jock. 'For three years I was top of every class; my results were fantastic. Mr Watt was an average student but nothing special, and Mr Prickly had promised me that foreman's job. Then, on the day of the final exams, everyone was struck down by a stomach bug. Everyone, except old Warty Watt.'

'Warty Watt? Is that what you called him?

'Yes, everybody called him Warty Watt. He has a big wart on his bottom. We all saw it in the showers after football practise one day. He was such a horrible boy that no one minded calling him Warty. Anyway, I was ill for my tests and spent the whole examination running to the toilet until the last time.........'

'Yes, Grandpa?'

'Until..... the last time, it was too late,' sighed Grandpa Jock, 'I tried to finish my exam but I ended up sitting in a pool of my own poo.'

'Urgh, what happened then, Mr Jock?'

'Well, of course, I failed my exams. Mr Watt got my job as foreman at the power plant and I felt so ashamed that I left the town to join the army.'

'You've nothing to be embarrassed about, Grandpa. Everybody has 'followed through' now and again, especially when they've been really ill.' said George reassuringly.

'And Mr Jock, you are a good man,' confirmed Allison, 'you're worth a hundred of old Warty Watt.' And all three of them laughed.

'You're right, lass.' said Grandpa Jock, pulling himself together. 'Now, it's payback time!'

*

While they'd been talking George had been thinking.

'Grandpa?' he asked, 'how did you escape from the exercise bike up there? Why weren't you drugged by the sludge, like everybody else?

'Well, I was to start with, lad, covered in all these blooming plasters but on Thursday, they dragged me oot o' here and strapped me onto one of them bikes, shoved a tube in my arm then used a control box to hoist me and the bike up to the ceiling. Said I had to work for my living.'

'That must have been terrible.' said Allison.

'No, lass. The worst bit was when they ripped all the plasters of me.' Grandpa Jock made a face and drew in air through his pursed lips. 'Ooh ya! That was painful.' he remembered.

'Weren't you scared being so high up?' asked George.

'It wasn't fun. My bike kept shaking around as I pedalled but I had to keep going or I would've been zapped.'

'So how did you get down?' asked George.

'Well, after aboot an 'oor o' pedalling, the two giants left me alone and I realised that the drugged tea and biscuit mixture wisnae being pumped up that high. I felt light-headed but I wisnae a zombie like those old yins doon on the ground,' explained Grandpa. 'so I reached into my shirt, pulled oot my little bagpipe repair kit and hot-wired the electricity. I used all the spare sludge tubes and the electric cable to slide down to the ground.'

'Why didn't you escape then?' asked Allison.

'Look around, lass. There are no windows in here and the doors were all locked so I tried to raise the alarm the only way I could think of.'

'Ah right!' exclaimed George, 'that's when I heard your bagpipes in the tunnel for the first time.'

'Spot on, boy. When I was searching around the factory floor I found the entertainment controls near the big biscuit mushing machine. I switched off the giant TV, plugged my little USB stick into the speaker system and turned the volume up full blast for a few seconds before they caught me. They hoisted me up even higher but at least they didn't find my little repair kit and I hoped someone would've heard my signal.'

'I did, Grandpa. In the tunnel when I was doing detention.'

'Then yesterday, I heard your reply and knew help was on its way.' Grandpa Jock winked again.

'We still weren't sure where you were,' said Allison, 'George played that music in the tunnel to see where the noise came out. I heard it when I was outside, coming from the power plant.'

'Aye, lad, you were lucky,' grinned Grandpa, 'the two big bruisers were cleaning out that little train and they had the tunnel doors open at this end. The noise of that pipe band flew out of the tunnel and filled this factory. I think the Basch brothers almost wet themselves with fright.'

'So the music I heard must have come out of the chimneys.' said Allison.

'That's right,' replied Grandpa Jock. 'you turned the tunnel, this factory and the three chimneys into a giant, acoustic set of bagpipes, George. I knew help would be coming so I just had to keep out of trouble and wait.'

'Sorry it's only us though, Grandpa,' said George sheepishly, 'some rescue squad we turned out to be.'

'That's okay, son. Two extra pairs of hands are all I'll need.'

XXII. PROS, CONS AND GONE

Mr Watt had returned to his office high above the factory floor and closed the door behind him, alone in his sumptuous suite. He snapped off his rubber gloves and tossed them into the bucket in the corner.

It was after 3 o'clock and he'd wasted his whole Saturday on those two miscreants. Mr Watt also hated being in his power plant in the afternoon. Soon the Basch Brothers would start their daily clean-out operations, flushing out the slop buckets from underneath three thousand bicycling bottoms and that was when his factory became rather atmospheric.

'Shame that it smells so. Everything else about my plant is simply brilliant.' he said to himself, as he strolled behind his desk and plonked his fat bottom into his fat, leather chair. He rocked back and forth on the springs, still talking.

'Efficient, self-sustaining, perpetual energy. Pump in, pump out. We don't even waste a drop of slop!'

Mr Watt smiled at his ingenuity. All the pedallers' waste was pumped into the large holding tank where it was allowed to continuously ferment and bubble, releasing methane gas to power the pod-train in the tunnel and the excess gas was flushed into a turbine where it was burned off as yet another source of energy. This method actually produced more heat and energy and far less carbon dioxide than burning other fossil fuels.

'Never mind old people,' he thought, 'If only I could get cows onto bikes...'

Then he thought about this recent turn of events. He'd never thought about kidnapping children before, maybe this was an opportunity. He took a scrap of paper and a pencil out of the bottom drawer of his desk and began to draw up a list. He wrote the words 'Pros' at the top of the page and underlined it. He wrote;

Pros

Longevity – can cycle for years

Don't eat as much as old people (to begin with)

Will get stronger as they grow

Smaller bikes – could squeeze more into the factory

Easier to catch

He paused for a moment as he thought, then he wrote;

Cons

Can't keep dumping their bikes at the edge of cliffs

They'll grow up and eat more (but will they pedal faster?)

May arouse suspicion – nobody worries about old people.

Parents, parents, parents!

'No,' Mr Watt muttered under his stale breath, 'more trouble than they're worth.' And he threw the pencil down on the desk. 'Why do parents worry about their children so much? Damn ungrateful, noisy little brats! Nobody ever worried about me like that and I turned out fine.'

He thought back to his own, empty childhood. His ragged clothes, the way the other children would torment him about his smell. It wasn't his fault that his mother had left him when he was a baby and his father drank too much to care. Mr Watt's happiest Christmas was when his father gave him a magnifying glass, which was a free gift with a bottle of whisky, and Mr Watt had spent many happy hours burning the wings off flies and frying other insects. That was when he'd learned the joy of power and control. He held the destiny of these little creatures in his hands; he could choose if they lived or died, wingless, legless, headless or fried.

Mr Watt had always hated the children who teased him at school. He hated the children who came into the burger bar where he first worked. They'd order burgers and chips and laugh at his silly paper hat so much that he'd have to spit in their buns.

That job in the burger bar was Mr Watt's first taste of real freedom, as well as his first taste of beef burgers, since he'd often gone hungry for days as a small child, and the burger bar allowed their staff to eat all the burgers that hadn't been sold. He grew to love 'dumped' burgers and would always eat as many as he possibly could. At first, they had no effect on his waistline but as his addiction to the greasy junk food continued after he married, all that fat began to pile up around his belly.

Although the burger bar didn't pay very much money, Mr Watt was able to use his wages to pay his way through Power Plant Academy and he was very good at saving his cash.

The burger bar job also paid for his first suit which, as soon as he put it on, made him feel powerful. A surge of energy would race through his veins every time he wore it; his shoulders would pull back, he stood straighter, taller and for the first time in his life, he felt proud. Proud that he'd worked hard to give himself a chance to get even with the world.

When he met Petunia Prickly, he found a woman who shared his hatred of small children and love of burgers. That was their first date. Mr Watt decided to show how classy he was by taking Miss Prickly to the burger bar and paying for their meal, as opposed to eating the dumped left-overs from the garbage bin. Strangely, Mr Watt often wondered, no matter how many burgers his wife ate, and she'd eaten thousands over the last thirty years, she never put on any weight. Petunia stayed thin and gaunt and actually always looked like she needed a good feed.

Now Mr Watt watched from his high office window as his skinny wife walked across the factory floor below to fit the feeding tubes into the arms of those brat-children. The only trouble was that when he looked further along to the end of the rows, the two machines allocated to George and Allison were empty, so was the exercise bike swinging high above the rest. Mr Watt's latest three recruits were gone.

They'd escaped!

XXIII. ESCAPE!

Grandpa Jock was also watching Mrs Watt walking across the factory floor, peering through a slim crack in the open storeroom door. At the same moment Mr Watt saw the empty exercise bikes, Grandpa Jock made his move.

He'd taken a baby blue tracksuit top from the store cupboard and was now rushing towards Mrs Watt from behind. He quickly wrapped the tracksuit around her head, plunging her into darkness and spun her around three times. He then pushed her across towards George and Allison shouting 'Sit on her!'

Mrs Watt was, by now, completely disorientated and had dropped the two hypodermic needles she had been carrying, clearly intended for use on the new inmates. She stumbled to the floor beside her two startled pupils, who were only too quick to jump on their teacher, happy to grind their bottoms onto her skinny frame and pinning her to the floor. George even tried to squeeze his bottom a little bit, hoping to fart on his teacher, but this time he was scared he'd follow through too.

'Search her pockets, lad,' shouted Grandpa Jock, 'find her bunch of keys!' and George patted her pockets, listening for any faint jingle.

Grandpa Jock was on the move again, running towards the end of the rows towards the stairs as fast as his short strides could carry him. George saw the urgency as Mr Watt had ran out of his office and along the balcony to the top of the stairs. He was now leaping down the steps two at a time, rushing to the rescue of his wife.

Grandpa Jock was just as quick. At the last column, he stopped and fumbled beneath the first bike. With a yank he pulled out the second of the brown tubes from underneath the pedaller. This wasn't the tea and biscuits tube, this was the coil from the slop bucket and the pressure from the overflowing Pooper Scooper Loop sprayed a large arc of dirty brown liquid towards the stairs and over the floor.

The old man ran to the next bike, releasing the filthy fluid again and to the next bike and the next. Soon the floor was awash with a dark brown sludgy gunge. Mr Watt had been too intent on saving his wife that he hadn't noticed the wet floor as he reach the bottom of the stairs. By the time the stench reached his nostrils and he'd planted his right foot on the factory floor, it was too late. He slipped in the sludge and went sliding across the surface, crashing straight into the first row of exercise bikes.

The cyclists were completely oblivious to this commotion, pedalling onwards through another episode of the Antiques Roadshow. Mr Watt's brown suit was now browner and dirtier than it had ever been before and he felt his stomach churn as the cold, wet slop seeped through the material and soaked his skin. He froze for a second in disgust and gagged as the foul smell forced its way up his nostrils. His suit was saturated in pensioner poop and...

Bang!

In Mr Watt's momentary loss of waste-related concentration, Grandpa Jock had broken off a pan from one of the oldest exercise bikes and seized the opportunity to take Warty Watt by surprise. Grandpa Jock smashed the metal bed pan across Mr Watt's head, splattering him with even more poo.

Mr Watt fell to the floor with a splash and Grandpa Jock ran back round to where George and Allison were still sitting on top of their teacher. George was proudly swinging a large bunch of keys from his finger.

'Good work, lad.' winked Grandpa Jock snatching the keys out of his hand. The surprisingly fast old Scotsman then ran around to the tea and biscuits pumping tank. After three failures, he opened the little hatch door at the bottom of the yellow console and pulled out a small black bullet-shaped object.

George watched intently as Grandpa Jock doubled back to the bikes and ripped a handful of tea and biscuit tubes (thankfully not the other tubes but since the floor was covered in stuff anyway, it probably wouldn't have made any difference) out from the back of the bikes and tied them onto the bottom of the stairs. Fixed at one end, he trailed the rest of the tubes over to the entertainment system next to the big mixing tanks. His hands moved quickly as he pushed buttons and turned dials. The giant screen flickered and went blank.

George saw that the black bullet in his Grandpa Jock's hand was his little USB stick. The memory stick that contained all of his favourite bagpipe music! Grandpa Jock stuck the stick into the socket and he fiddled with the console again. Three seconds later...

BOOM, BOOM, BOOM!'

Eeeoowweeeyyeeoohhhheeyyyoowwwwwwwwww!

The factory floor was now filled with the sound of a thousand cats being simultaneously strangled whilst cannons were being constantly fired to keep the kitten killers in time with the rhythm.

BOOM BOOM BOOM Eeeohheyyooow

BOOM BOOM BOOM Eeeohoyyooww!

The pipes and drums from Grandpa Jock's favourite regimental band pounded out a purposeful tune at the loudest volume setting that Grandpa Jock could find. Allison covered her ears and George's brain began to bounce around again, as it had done down in the tunnel a couple of days before.

'Is it really time for music, Grandpa?' shouted George, straining to be heard over the pipes and drums.

'Watch this, laddie!' replied Grandpa Jock, grinning and slowly at first, the old pedallers began to look around them. The glazed, vacant expression that they'd all had across their faces was beginning to lift as the booming music began to cut through their drug-induced stupor.

'Attention, auld yins,' bellowed Grandpa Jock in his most fearsome sergeant-major's voice. 'rip the yellow tube out of your arms - NOW!' he ordered and George saw that many of the old people were looking bemused at the back of their hands. Some of them actually started pulling at the tubes and a few of them succeeded in freeing themselves from the tea and biscuit drip.

When they did this, George and Allison could see the old people begin to give themselves a shake as the flow of sedative was removed from their bodies. Surprisingly quickly, and perhaps helped by the bagpipes screaming in their ears, awareness returned to the freed pedallers and they began pulling the tubes out from the arms of their more doped-up neighbours.

More and more old people were awakening from their comatose condition but amazingly, they continued to pedal, as fast and as furious as they had always done. Maybe it just came naturally to them now, maybe their legs were programmed to pedal or maybe there was still a fear of electric shock embedded in their heads. Whatever it was, they couldn't help themselves.

'Attention, auld yins.' bellowed Sergeant-Major Jock again. 'On my command, STOP PEDALLING!' and to George's astonishment, most of the ancient cyclists obeyed immediately. Their legs were frozen in mid-pedal and for the first time in years, their perpetual motion ceased and hundreds and hundreds legs were captured in suspended animation.

Time stood still. George held this petrified scene before his eyes for an everlasting second. Then the little lights on the front of each bike dropped from green to amber to red. Electric currents zapped around the factory floor, electrifying cyclist after cyclist and dozens of white haired heads began bobbing around as the shocks became more intense and the smoke began to pour out of the front of some of the bikes.

What didn't happen was pedalling. Not one of the elderly cyclists began to pedal again. Clearly they were all now drug-free and sensing their freedom, and they were all fighting against the 12 volt motivation that was surging through their bodies, encouraging them to start pedalling again.

It was one of the bikes at the front, near where George and Allison were still sitting on top of their teacher, that was first to blow. There was a massive explosion of sparks and smoke and the handlebars of the exercise bike flew straight up into the air.

The punishment circuit had been overloaded by the huge increase in stubborn cyclists refusing to cycle; designed only to deal with the occasional offender and not to cope with en-masse stoppages. The surge of electric energy to so many bikes had short-circuited the system and the bikes were now free from the voltage source. The ever-more responsive pensioners were now clawing at the leather straps and shackles around their ankles.

George was taking heart from his Grandpa Jock's commanding performance. 'Now get out of here!' ordered George at the top of his voice.

However, this distraction had given Mrs Watt, who had been sitting quietly biding her time, the opportunity to catch the children off guard, pushing them aside and rolling out from underneath them. She pulled the blue tracksuit from off her head and the mad music burst into her ears louder than before. In a state of shock, she stopped to press her hands over her ears.

Mr Watt had picked himself up and was now absolutely furious. 'Leave the old fogeys, they can't escape. The main door's locked. Get those three!'

It was at that point that Mrs Watt was hit with a second surprise. The handlebars from the exercise bike that had exploded were now obeying the laws of gravity and plummeting back to earth. Unfortunately for Mrs Watt, she was between the handlebars and the ground and they hit her hard on the top of her head, knocking her straight onto the floor.

Recovering from Mrs Watt's sudden escape and taking advantage of the help from the handlebars, George and Allison ran around to the back of the block of bikes.

Grandpa Jock looked as if he was enjoying himself, running towards the tubes tied to the stairs and grabbing hold of them. A split second later, the Basch Brothers burst through the door at the bottom of the stairs, alerted by the blaring music but this time not surprised by it. They thought they knew what to expect.

What did surprise them was when Grandpa Jock pulled hard on the tubes and a tangled mess of pipes wrapped tightly around their ankles. They tried to run, only succeeding in tripping then stumbling into the centre of the room. Their next shock followed shortly afterwards as they splashed down into the filthy, smelly puddles pouring over the floor. Grandpa Jock had used the tubes as a tripwire and the Basch brothers were now doing the breaststroke in the brown stuff.

Grandpa Jock dropped the tubes and met George and Allison at the back of the bikes.

'What will we do now, Grandpa?' shouted George, aware that a doo-doo drenched Mr Watt was staggering to his feet and the muck stained brothers were lurching around on their hands and knees towards them. Once again, their hands were stained brown but this time it wasn't from the tea-bags. It was even caked underneath their fingernails!

'Mrs Watt's coming too.' yelled Allison, pointing to the other side of the exercise bikes, where the mad-eyed teacher had picked up the two syringes and was blocking their path.

Grandpa Jock's eyes were darting left and right. The exercise bikes were too tightly packed to safely run through and their angry captors were closing in. Grandpa Jock looked up. His bike was dangling on its platform 10 metres above their heads.

'There's nowhere left for you to run, old man,' growled a wet, sludgy Mr Watt, 'best return quietly and rejoin the production line.'

'Pull the poo tubes.' ordered Grandpa Jock and he tugged the brown coil out of the slop bucket from the bike in front of him. George and Allison did the same, ripping and tugging at all the tubing they could get their hands on. Grandpa Jock turned and grabbed the yellow control box below his bike. He pushed the green buttons marked 'Down' and the platform above them began to descend.

The Basch boys and the Watts realised what was happening but continued their slow, impending march towards them, every inch of their evil bodies covered from head to toe in foul, smelling waste. Mr Watt was waddling, with his fat belly swinging from side to side as he stepped through the puddles. He hadn't even had time to put his rubber gloves on, not that it would've mattered.

The platform stopped just above the ground.

'Jump on!' yelled Grandpa Jock and he climbed aboard his chain-mounted exercise bike. George and Allison stopped pulling tubes and stepped onto the platform, holding tightly onto the handlebars. Grandpa Jock pressed the button marked 'Up' and they rose up towards the ceiling. When they were safely beyond the reach of the four advancing maniacs, Grandpa Jock pushed the red 'Stop' button and the lurching platform stopped and began to gently swing back and forth.

Below them Mr Watt was grinning fiendishly. He pointed to one of the Basch brothers, then to the entertainment console. Either Boris or Buster, George didn't know the difference, walked over and pulled the black USB stick out of its socket. The room fell silent but for the ringing in everyone's ears.

Mr Watt's eyes flashed and Allison gasped at the crazed look in his face. He spoke softly but his voice was filled with venom. 'There is nowhere left to run. You will be pulled down or you will fall down,' hissed the power plant director, 'either way, I shall have you.'

Mr Watt looked down at his muck strewn hands, wiped them across his balloon of a belly and then returned his gaze up at the helpless threesome on the swinging platform. 'Your punishment will greatly surpass your actions. Discipline will be returned.'

XXIV. FLOOD

Up above the smelly villains, George began to impersonate his Grandpa Jock, using his best Sergeant-Major's voice. George shouted 'Swing!' and he began throwing his weight to and fro on the platform, holding onto the chains securing the bike to the ceiling. The bike began to swing backwards and forwards.

Grandpa Jock and Allison were clutching on desperately but began to bend their knees, pushing their weight towards the wall then releasing to allow the platform to fall backwards.

Soon, the three of them had pushed enough momentum into the platform that the bike was now swinging high above the other exercise bikes then back towards the wall, arcing above the tunnel and above the black septic tank. The two Watts and the two Basch boys could only watch helplessly, slightly puzzled and growing more annoyed that their troublesome captives were still hoping to escape.

George then whispered, 'Right, you two. When I say 'jump', we all jump. Okay?'

'Where to, George?' gasped Allison. 'There's nowhere to go.'

'There! I see it too.' said Grandpa Jock, pointing towards the narrow gap built into the wall between the low ceiling and the top of the large septic tank.

'But what if there's no way out from there, George?' complained Allison, wondering if George and his Grandpa were thinking clearly.

'We don't need to get out yet, lass.' replied the old Scotsman and before anyone could discuss the situation further, George shouted 'Jump!' right at the platform's highest arc, above the black tank.

The three of them flew through the air, aiming for the narrow gap in the wall and miraculously they all made it. Allison almost lost her footing but George and Grandpa Jock both grabbed her at the same time and hauled her safely onto the tank.

The space between the top of the tank and ceiling was low, but just high enough for them to stand stooped, hunching their backs and shoulders. On top of the tank were a number of pipes and levers, as well as a large crank handle which stood next to a shiny, stainless steel gate valve. The valve looked like a big steering wheel and was painted bright red.

'What're you doing, Grandpa?' whispered George. He wasn't sure why he was whispering because the Basch brothers and the Watts were closing in on the tank, still looking as menacing as anyone can be while dripping in poo.

'I figured it out when I was up on that bike,' Grandpa Jock spat out, 'It's simple really. Just a case of reversing the plumbing.' He was working feverishly now, un-clipping valves and reconnecting pipes. The last one he screwed in place was the largest and it pointed back into the tunnel. Grandpa Jock grabbed the crank handle and pulled it back in the opposite direction. There was a loud hiss and a rumble beneath their feet.

'Bring them down, boys,' shouted Mr Watt, who was now standing at the base of the tank. 'throw them down, if you have to.'

'They're coming up the ladder!' squealed Allison. George hadn't noticed before but there was a ladder, poorly welded onto the end of the tank. The rivets looked old and rusty and there was a safety cage surrounding the ladder to form a tube, up which the Basch brothers were now climbing. These were big guys, with broad shoulders and barrel chests and the ladder's cage wasn't designed to fit such chunky climbers. The cramped conditions didn't stop them, merely slowed them down.

George looked down over the edge and saw the first of the Basch boys climbing hand over hand, one rung at a time, cautiously approaching. His muck splattered face grimaced up at George and when their eyes met, the burly henchman stopped climbing and he drew his thumb across his throat with a tearing, scratching noise. George jumped back, remembering the shadow from the black, floating truck.

'Nearly there, lad,' grunted Grandpa Jock, 'give us a hand, you two.' And the three off them began to twist the red wheel to open the valve. It was very stiff but after the first jerky yank, the wheel turned with a squeak and soon they were spinning the wheel furiously.

Just as the wheel clunked to fully open the valve, the first smelly brown head popped up at the top of the ladder. The Basch brothers were getting closer and closer, and to Allison and George it looked a long way down.

Down!

Back down on the factory floor, George and Allison saw the most unbelievable sight. Grandpa Jock raised his hand, pointing at the incredible scene. His bottom jaw wavered up and down, silently mouthing his amazement. Even the head of the uppermost Basch boy was turned towards the drama unfolding on the factory floor. No doubt the Basch brother below was also transfixed on the ladder.

'Go on, ma beauties!' shouted Grandpa Jock, elated at the elderly victory going on below.

The Watts, who had been standing at the base of the black tank, had now been engulfed by a swarm of irate oldies, who had clearly gained their own composure and a growing sense of injustice. There were hundreds of them, a sea of balding heads and white candy-floss hair, wearing pink and baby blue tracksuits, buzzing all over the floor and taking it in turns to kick the Watts up the bottom as they were now bent over a couple of exercise bikes.

Some of those beautifully aimed bottom blows looked rather painful, George reckoned, since the over-developed leg muscles of some of the most experienced cyclists could drop kick a cow through a barn door.

The look of menace and mischief had disappeared from the visible Basch brother's face as he slowly weighed up whether it was safer to stay quietly up on top of the tank or to risk the wrath of the wrinklies back on the ground, and potentially be over-powered by the provoked pensioners.

It was not a difficult choice. Boris, or Buster, started to climb to the top of the ladder, indicating to his brother Buster, or Boris, that they should take cover in a dark corner, hidden away from the baying mob of lavender talcum powder and thinning hair.

If only things were that simple. As both the Basch brothers climbed higher up the ladder, the more stress their weight put on the old and rusty rivets holding the ladder in place. At the very top, just as the uppermost thug was about to put his boot onto the tank, he lost his footing and slipped back. Luckily for him, he was supported by the safety cage which stopped him from falling backwards completely.

Unluckily for him, and his brother below, that was all the pressure the rivets could take and they popped loose with a metallic snap. The ladder and the safety cage fell backwards, leaving the henchmen hanging at a desperate angle. George rushed towards the ladder and gave the cage an extra push. They dropped again but their descent was halted by another set of rivets further below. The added pressure onto those rusty, old bolts soon caused them to sheer off and plummet the ladder further.

And that's how the Russians reached the ground; bouncing, falling, jerking and breaking down to the factory floor, their descent gaining more and more momentum until the caged ladder smacked against the ground. It was soon swarmed over by a horde of enormously muscled legs who began jumping all over the safety cage, crushing it down tight and occasionally sticking a boot into the ribs of the Russians who were lying helplessly trapped in their metal snare.

Now whilst this amazing scene had been unfolding, Grandpa Jock had remembered why he'd been reversing the plumbing and pipes. Grandpa Jock was certain that there would be an exit hatch inside the tank, leading to the outside. The tank had to be emptied somehow. Mr Watt had said that he sold the filthy stuff to farmers as fertiliser so there had to be an escape hatch in there but he didn't fancy swimming through the poo to find it. He'd been hoping to flush out the slurry tank before going in, especially since the fumes would be quite noxious and probably highly flammable as well.

Grandpa Jock looked over the edge of the tank, towards the tunnel and saw the effectiveness of his plan. A great, gushing torrent of thick brown sludge was thundering out of the tank and roaring back down the tunnel towards the school. The little magnetic pod was nowhere to be seen; Mr Jolly had taken it when he returned to lock everything up and a river of slimy slush was now flooding towards him.

'How do we get down now, Grandpa?' panicked George, realising their predicament, 'The ladder's gone.'

'I'm not sure, lad,' said Grandpa Jock, rubbing his chin, 'I'm making this up as I go along.' His plan to escape through the sludge tank didn't seem quite so clever now, once he'd seen the fury at which the muck was flushing out of the pipe at the bottom.

'One ladder coming up, Jock, you old codger!' shouted a voice from below.

'Hey, that's old Harry Higginbottom! I thought he was off sailing round the world.' spluttered Grandpa Jock and they watched as about twenty old men formed a circle, bent their knees and squatted, their thick thighs pressing tightly against their neighbours.

Then another crowd of elderly gents climbed on top of the squatters, standing securely on the firm thighs of the bottom row.

As soon as they second layer of antiquated acrobats were in position another rush of oldies clambered up to form the next level.

'They're building a human pyramid, Mr Jock,' yelled Allison, pointing, 'I've seen this on the TV.'

As each layer of the ladder was added, the pyramid became narrower and narrower, with fewer and fewer aged stuntmen climbing up to the next level. Within seconds, the tower was almost to the top of the tank with about five or six levels of senior supporters holding the structure firm. George was amazed at how firm the tower looked, there was no shaking or wobbling, it was absolutely rock solid. Muscles, strengthened by years of exercise and growth supplements, had provided the former prisoner pedallers with the ideal platform to rescue the rescuers.

Grandpa Jock was the first to leap down, placing his feet securely onto the thighs of a grinning geriatric, who was missing most of his teeth. Grandpa Jock held out his hand and helped Allison step onto another toothless senior's leg, then lowering her down to the next level. There were hands reaching out at every stage to guide and support her, solid in their stance, comforting in their steady reassurance.

George followed closely behind, even beginning to catch Allison up as he descended down around the other side of the pensioners' pyramid. Grandpa Jock was quickly hopping from thigh to thigh; keen to get back on firm ground again. And as Grandpa Jock moved off the upper levels, those men at the top cascaded down to the thighs of their buddies below.

Allison and George reached the floor of the former power plant at the same time, closely followed by an excited Grandpa Jock, and then the rest of their rescuers began spilling down onto the ground again. There were handshakes and back slapping all round as George, Allison and Grandpa Jock thanked the tower of golden oldies, who in turn thanked them for freeing them from their pedal prison. The oldest inmates, the ones with the largest muscles, had been cycling for over five years, many of them the original passengers on the first bus-load that went missing, presumed heading for Africa.

The Watts were securely tied across the saddles of two exercise bikes and the Basch boys were rolled up in a metal cage that once was the septic tank's ladder. It had been crushed and twisted like a giant Christmas cracker by the thunderous thighs of the elderly. The four maniacs were going nowhere.

George's nostrils twitched. The stench back down on the ground was absolutely disgusting and there were pools of pee and poo slopping around the back of almost every bike, where the tubes had been ripped out by the angry mob. George glanced across and saw that the slurry was still flooding out of the giant septic tank and flooding down the tunnel. He wondered, what would happen when it reached Mr Jolly's basement?

George didn't want to wait to find out. Taking the old boys and girls by surprise, after all they were still celebrating their freedom; George sprinted across to the large tunnel door, built big enough to protect a bank vault and threw himself against it. His weight hardly moved the door but his momentum and scraping feet soon began to push the door closed. It shut with a loud clanging echo and George swirled the locking wheel around and around, blocking out the filthy sediment flowing down to the school.

XXV. THE DANGERS OF SMOKING

Earlier, Mr Jolly had returned to the boiler room in the magnetic pod-train. It had shot down the tunnel, always faster going back downhill to the school than the slow climb back up.

Mr Jolly had locked the main school gates and the doors. He'd checked that there was absolutely no sign of those children ever having visited the school that morning. He'd locked his boiler room door from the inside and had returned past the tea-bag and the teeth cupboard to the dark room with the 'lost property' cabinets and a vault door.

He was about to take the pod back up to the power plant when he decided that he deserved a cigarette. He was the one doing all the hard work after all; that lot up there only had to babysit a couple of kids and a bunch of drugged-up, tied-up old codgers. So leaving the vault door open he stepped back into the tea-bag room, sparked his lighter and lit up a cigarette.

As the foul smoke cleared, Mr Jolly was about to take another draw on his cigarette when a new odour entered his nostrils. Even though his sense of smell had been almost destroyed by years of polluting his nasal passages with nicotine, this was a pungent, almost over-powering stench, almost recognisable as the foul odour he'd experienced slopping out the old generators this week when those 'lazy Russians' were complaining about their 'injuries'.

Mr Jolly's nostrils twitched and he turned his head towards the green door. The smell was definitely coming from the cabinet room. He walked through slowly and stuck his head round the corner. The vault door was open and the stale stink was certainly stronger in here. Mr Jolly stepped towards the vault door, now having to cover his mouth and nose with his arm. He could hear a constant rushing noise, like a distant waterfall, only this waterfall was getting nearer and nearer. The whooshing noise was getting louder and the vile tang was getting stronger.

The far-from-jolly janitor stepped into the tunnel, at the top of the steps and the surging, flooding noise echoed around him. The putrid smell hit him in the face like a cricket bat.

In the almost darkness, Mr Jolly peered up the tunnel. Then, in split second there came a torrent of brown sludge slammed into the metal staircase and the small train sitting on the magnetic rail. Like a sewer without an overflow pipe, the mucky scum sloshed around the stairs and floor of the tunnel, the initial impact knocking Mr

Jolly backwards, his pink wellington boots slipping on the wet surface.

At first, the janitor thought he was going to fall but he thrust his hand out and caught the grab-rail just in time. In doing so, his burning cigarette dropped out of his hand and fell downwards, twirling end over end. Just before the red hot tip hit the sludgy ooze, a spark flicked into the noxious gases of methane, hydrogen sulphide and ammonia that had been bubbling up from the flooding mush and caught light, causing the atmosphere to explode in a massive eruption of fumes.

A giant fireball roared back upwards through the tunnel, following the surface of the brown river, and reached the vault door at the top. George had just been able to shut this in time, effectively sealing off the tunnel, trapping the igniting gas inside. With nowhere to escape to and the build up of fumes from the flushing valve adding more fuel to the raging inferno, pressure forced the fireball back down the tunnel to where the methane storage tank that fuelled the train had already been damaged.

The second explosion was about 100 times bigger than the first!

XXVI. STRANGE RAIN

The power plant was rocked by the first explosion, the ground shook and even the sturdiest legged pensioner staggered to keep their balance.

George yelled, 'Out this way, follow me!' And he ran past the bikes to the door where the Basch Brothers had come in and Allison followed. Flooding behind came a procession of the old and the elderly, far from being frail most of them were now fit and muscular, easily keeping up with the sprinting young legs of George and Allison.

George and Grandpa Jock quickly wedged open the double doors and a bottleneck of blue and pink tracksuits built up around the exit. Instead of pushing and shoving and fighting for freedom, the crowd was afflicted by a dangerous outbreak of good manners. Rather than ploughing through the open doors, elderly gentlemen would take a step backwards...

'After you, sir.'

'No sir, after you.'

'But I insist.'

'Ladies first, gentlemen.'

This sudden rash of politeness could've been catastrophic for the evacuation had the cure not been delivered in the guise of the second explosion. The whole power plant shook violently and a booming rumble rocked the walls and floor.

There wasn't exactly a stampede towards the door; remnants of politeness still remained in the elderly crowd but there was an orderly surge to the outside world. Grandpa Jock and George led the way pulling open the lobby doors and sunlight shone into the pale pensioners' faces for the first time in a long time. Blinking and shielding their eyes from the glare of the sun, hundreds and hundreds of the ex-geriatric generators poured out of the doors, spilling across the large courtyard behind the high metal wall that shielded the power plant from the outside world.

'Get the main gate, lad.' urged Grandpa Jock and George and Allison ran towards the large double gates at the bottom of the entrance road. Most of the old inmates had been trapped in the factory for years, so they really did have a great deal of difficulty adjusting their eyes to the natural daylight and they stumbled around the courtyard. Even Grandpa Jock, having only been inside for less than a week was partially blinded by the low evening sunshine. George and Allison weaved their way through the throng and pulled back a series of long bolts across the middle of the gates and another two penetrating the ground. The gates opened outwards to the grassy parkland that George and Allison had cycled around the previous day. So much had happened since then, was it really just the previous day?

Allison and George were first to walk off power plant property. The view over the town was as breathtaking as ever but the two friends weren't interested in the landscape. There was a large plume of thick, black smoke rising from a deep hole in the ground at the bottom of the hill.

A blast crater had been formed where their school had once stood!

There was absolutely nothing left of their school; it had been completely demolished in the gas explosion. The main building, the primary block and Mr Jolly's workshop and boiler room were all gone, replaced by a smouldering hole in the ground. It was at least 3 metres deep and 100 metres across. The pensioners of Little Pumpington were now flowing out through the power plant with looks of shock and amazement splashed across their faces.

Grandpa Jock, eyes slowly adjusting, walked across to George and put his hand on his grandson's shoulder and laughed, 'You've blown up your school. Well done, lad.'

'I, I, I d-didn't mean to, Grandpa,' stammered George, 'will I be in trouble for it?

'I shouldn't think so, lad' reassured Grandpa Jock, 'those four in there are in a lot more trouble. And anyway, isn't it every schoolboy's dream to blow up their school? Enjoy it, lad. You're living the dream!'

Then, plop.

Plop, plop, plop.

'Ooh ya!'

Something hit Grandpa Jock on his head.

'Ooh ya!' and again.

'Ow!' shouted George, as he was struck from above too.

'Ouch, I've been bitten!' screeched Allison.

George knew exactly what it was. All around them old people were ducking for cover as little pink and white objects splattered down around them. It was raining false teeth!

Some of the false teeth smashed on the hard tarmac. Some sets landed safety on the grass and some falsers managed to hit more of the old people.

'It's the false teeth from Mr Jolly's cupboard,' exclaimed George in astonishment, 'Grandpa, what are you doing?'

Grandpa Jock was crawling around on the grass, picking up different pairs of false teeth and putting them in his mouth.

'Nope, too big,' he muttered to himself, 'Nope, too small. A-ha, these will do!' And he popped a top set onto his old gums. 'Right, let's find the bottom half,' and he was soon scrambling about on all fours, desperately searching for teeth.

'Urgh, Grandpa,' groaned George, 'they could be anybodies!'

'But they could also be mine,' argued Grandpa Jock, 'and if they fit, that's all that matters.'

Grandpa Jock continued, 'And another thing, I'm ninety three, you know.'

Grandpa Jock was joined by dozens of other oldies, trying out different pairs of false teeth for size, some happy with the fit, others tossing unsuitable choppers over their shoulders and continuing their search. Allison could see the look of desperate joy on their faces, anticipating their first proper meal, like steak pie, or fish and chips or something they would have to chew instead of being force-fed mushy digestive biscuits.

George turned and saw smoke rising out of the three tall chimney stacks at the back of the factory for the first time in years. Then he heard the wail of police sirens approaching the crater. And fire engines, and ambulances. All of them were not really necessary. The school sat safely in its own grounds and the explosion hadn't caused damage to any other buildings, apart from the school. The fires had blown themselves out in the explosion and all that was left smouldering in the crater were a few old mangled desks and singed text books blowing around the burnt hole that used to be the playground.

A siren's squeal was closer now and George saw a fleet of police cars racing up the windy road towards the power plant.

The Chief of Police was first to arrive. George sniggered at the look of complete and utter bewilderment on his face when he was confronted by hundreds of old people with over-developed limbs bursting out of their pretty pink and baby blue tracksuits, crawling around on the grass, sharing their false teeth and gumilly smiling at each other.

Allison leaned over and whispered in George's ear, 'This will take a lot of explaining.'

George just smiled.

XXVII. BACK ON TRACK

For the next 6 months the country was gripped by the unfolding story of Little Pumpington and Mr and Mrs Watt's mad scheme to create the cleanest, greenest and certainly meanest power plant in the whole world.

Other power plant owners wanted to know the secrets of their greedy counterpart's plans but were deterred from copying his evil scheme when Mr Watt was sentenced to 15,000 years imprisonment for the kidnap, wrongful imprisonment and the unwarranted prescription of illegal drugs to 3,284 people, as well as unlicensed storage of methane, the unlicensed storage and sale of untreated sewage, the false sale of over-priced utilities (i.e. electricity) and the grand theft of thousands of sets of false teeth, watches and walking sticks.

Mrs Watt also went on trial, charged with the same crimes. She tried to blame Mr Watt who, in turn, tried to blame Mrs Watt, but then Mrs Watt pleaded insanity, which George heartily agreed could've been the case.

For a few days, in the middle of the trials, it looked like Mrs Watt would be declared criminally insane and the whole blame would be put on her, leaving Mr Watt to get off scot-free. In the end, Mr Watt, as Managing Director of 3P's Power, was found guilty on all charges, as well as a few new ones which were added.

Mrs Watt, as sole share holder and owner of 3P's Power, was told by the court psychiatrist that she was not mad, just really, really bad and dangerous to know, but the judge took pity on her and only jailed her for 10,000 years, roughly 3000 jail sentences of 3 years each to run consecutively.

The people of Little Pumpington were thoroughly ashamed of themselves when they realised how easily they had been conned by the Watts, and how their antisocial behaviour had allowed the wickedest crimes to go unnoticed for over 5 years.

The mayor, in an effort to restore faith in the community, ran adverts in every national newspaper apologising for the town's lack of morale judgement and good conscience. He also mentioned that Little Pumpington had been no different from any other town in the country, until they had been led astray by the deceitful words and actions of a small group of people and that this should serve as a lesson to every good town in the land.

George was hailed as a hero for his quick thinking and bravery in the face of a daunting and seriously deranged enemy. Allison too, and the pair of them had their photos on the television, across the internet and in every newspaper. All the articles called him 'General George' for the commanding way he delivered his troops from danger.

No one called him 'Gorgeous George' ever again; George's Geriatric Army would never stand for it, so proud and protective were the pensioners of their rescuer.

For a while, the other power plant owners profited from the closure of the Little Pumpington's power plant. With no energy being produced locally, electricity was shipped in from around the national grid and the fat cats got a little fatter.

But the mayor and the people of Little Pumpington had learned plenty of lessons from their blinkered existence and had vowed to set a better example to themselves and everyone else.

The first thing they did was to dismantle the power plant, taking apart the exercise bikes and installing them in every house and home in the town. Now, if an overweight child or adult wanted to watch TV, or play a video game they had to pedal whilst they were doing it, to generate enough energy to power the television.

There was enough work for everyone who'd been employed in the old power plant, whether they picked their nose, or not. Jobs were aplenty as Little Pumpington took their lessons of hard work and exercise around the country.

And soon, Little Pumpington's newly built school had the fittest school children in the country and were always winning trophies, cups and rosettes at regional and national sports days, competitions and events. It was easy now that they'd found the proper role models.

Other businesses in the town began to see the benefits of having healthier employees, whilst at the same time, cutting back on their over-reliance on fossil fuels, which also saved them money, as Grandpa Jock said, 'Big businesses only care aboot big bucks.'

All the supermarkets put exercise bikes at every one of their checkouts so that the check-out operator had to pedal to move the conveyor belt bringing forward that customers shopping. It was hard for them at first, and check-out operators hated shoppers with lots of heavy tins of beans or multipacks, but the staff soon got used to it and became fitter into the bargain.

Petrol stations also installed exercise bikes on their forecourts to encourage lazy motorists to get out of their cars and work up an invigorating sweat now and again. Whenever drivers wanted to fill their cars up with petrol, they had to get on the exercise bike and pedal hard enough to pump the fuel into their own cars.

But to begin with, the elderly ex-cyclists of Little Pumpington weren't too sure what to do with their over-enhanced muscles. They were worried that if they went back to their old ways of no exercise, watching telly all day and shuffling back and forth to the shops, their powerful legs would shrink back to the withered limbs they used to have. So a plan was put into action.

Because of their fame, some of the old people wanted to become fitness instructors for all the old people of the country and they travelled far and wide to promote a message of health and fitness for everybody no matter what age they were.

Other old men rediscovered their football skills; it had been years since they'd enjoyed kicking a ball around the park. So good were they, and so powerful were their legs that they all signed up for a brand new football team called Oldman Athletic and they won the League Championship in their first season.

Other old people took up more sedate past-times. Some of them became professional dog walkers, taking people's dogs for long walks in the countryside. Soon the dogs were as fit as they'd ever been and able to keep up with the jogging geriatrics.

Not wishing to return to their bad old ways of burning smelly old fossil fuels, the townsfolk combined their exercise bikes with windmills built from the steel walls of the power plant. Everyone wanted a windmill to power their homes and they were a common site at the bottom of every garden. People even got used to the splattered remains of the odd seagull that flew too close to the spinning blades.

Next, wind farms and wave machines were built off the coast of Little Pumpington capturing the natural energy that was generated by stormy weather down by the seaside. The only energy that the inhabitants of Little Pumpington didn't harness was solar power. This was the north east of England, after all.

The Basch brothers began to repay their debt to society by cleaning up the power plant. Even though they worked as hard as they could, particularly because they wanted to get out of that foul smelling cesspit as quickly as possible, it still took them six months to hose down, clean, disinfect and polish the power plant. They spent almost the first three months of their sentence up to their knees in sh......... shocking amounts of filth.

But they knew they deserved it and worked hard to clean the power plant back to a usable condition. Of course, by then it was just a shell of a building since the old equipment had been removed years ago by Mr Watt and the exercise bikes had been recycled (if you pardon the pun) for home use.

And what better to turn an empty metal shell of a building into? A gigantic cinema, obviously, with a 180 degree screen reaching round three of the walls. Mr Watt hadn't been kidding about his state of the art sound system! With impressive 3-D cameras positioned up on the gantry outside Mr Watt's old office and rows and rows of plush cinema seats replacing the bikes that had once stood there, the power plant became the Film Factory and was filled every night by movie goers desperate to soak up the new (and better smelling) atmosphere of the surround sound 3-D theatre.

Almost a year after George had uncovered the giant geriatric generator and put an end to its slavery, he was sitting in the wooden glade at the bottom of his Grandpa's cul-de-sac. Allison was perched on the wooden tree trunk beside him.

'Our new teacher's nice.' she said, trying to break the silence.

'Yeah.' nodded George.

'And I'm glad we're into the new buildings, instead of those horrible porta-cabins.' she added.

'Yeah.' replied George.

'What's the matter, George?' asked Allison.

'Oh you know,' said George sadly, 'I miss my Grandpa Jock.'

Allison nodded solemnly. 'I know,' she said, 'but the old goat would go off on a round the world concert tour, playing his bagpipes to theatres and stadiums in twenty different countries, wouldn't he?'

George laughed. The thought of thousands of people paying good money to listen to his Grandpa Jock try to kill a cat was rather amusing.

'Still, he'll be back next month,' prompted Allison, 'and he promised he'd teach us that trick he tried once with the stink bombs, the fireworks, the tomato sauce and the Barbie dolls.'

George laughed again. Trust Grandpa Jock to think up a prank that could empty a shopping centre, call out the bomb squad and make a bunch of cute little dolls look like a scene from a zombie movie.

He'd only tried it once and of course, he was caught, since he wasn't as fast at running away as the rest of his speedy pensioner pals. But he was let off with a quiet caution,

Grandpa Jock being the hero of Little Pumpington and all. It was good time to keep his 'heid doon' for a bit; he called up the concert promoter who'd been badgering him to perform live, so desperate was he to show off the World's most famous 74 year old, or 81 or 93 year old.

'Do you think they'll ever find him?' asked Allison, changing the subject.

'What's left of him, you mean,' replied George. 'we've probably been breathing in tiny particles of Mr Jolly the Janitor for the last year.'

'But if he was blown up in the blast,' continued Allison, 'why did the police find his wellington boots, smouldering at the top of Plummet Point?'

'Maybe they were blown up and fell from the sky, like the false teeth?' guessed George.

'What? Neatly, sitting together, as a pair? I think he's still out there.'

George laughed.

'Jolly good show, Allison Wonderland.'

THE END

ABOUT THE AUTHOR

Stuart Reid is 43 years old, going on 14. Throughout his early life he was dedicated to being immature, having fun and getting into trouble. Occasionally, after scoring a goal in the playground Stuart was known to celebrate by kissing lollypop ladies, and he once broke his nose by running into a lamp-post with his jumper pulled up over his head. Although not musically gifted, Stuart has the ability to play music using only the pumping noises from his armpits.

Stuart once lobbied the British Olympic Committee to have 'The Wedgie' recognised as a national sport, creating both the 'Giving' and 'Receiving' categories and the scoring system with (skid) marks for technical merit, artistic impression and the durability/rippability of the underwear.

He is allergic to ties; blaming them for stifling the blood flow to his imagination throughout his twenties and thirties. Stuart was forced to spend the next 25 years being boring, professional and corporate. His fun-loving attitude was further suppressed by the weight of *career responsibility*, as a business manager in the retail and hospitality industries in the UK and Dubai.

Stuart's legs suffer from SAD (seasonal affective disorder) which means he has to wear shorts at all times. His midlife crisis offered a return to immature madness involving bogies, bums, burps, songs about poo and running about his snow covered garden in only his pyjamas.

Stuart has been married for nearly twenty years. He has two children, a superman outfit and a spiky haircut.

GORGEOUS GEORGE
AND THE GIANT GERIATRIC GENERATOR

BY STUART REID

PUBLISHED BY MY LITTLE BIG TOWN LTD 2011
WWW.MYLITTLEBIGTOWN.COM

ILLUSTRATIONS AND COVER ART BY
CALVIN INNES
WWW.CALVININNES.COM

FOR MORE GORGEOUS GEORGE GO TO:
WWW.MYLITTLEBIGTOWN.COM/GORGEOUSGEORGE